Carroll Davidson Wright, William Olin Atwater

Food Consumption

Carroll Davidson Wright, William Olin Atwater

Food Consumption

ISBN/EAN: 9783337122782

Printed in Europe, USA, Canada, Australia, Japan

Cover: Foto ©Andreas Hilbeck / pixelio.de

More available books at **www.hansebooks.com**

FOOD CONSUMPTION.

QUANTITIES, COSTS, AND NUTRIENTS

OF

FOOD-MATERIALS.

[FROM THE SEVENTEENTH ANNUAL REPORT OF THE
MASSACHUSETTS BUREAU OF STATISTICS
OF LABOR, pp. 239–328.]

BY

CARROLL D. WRIGHT,

CHIEF OF THE BUREAU OF STATISTICS OF LABOR.

CHEMICAL ANALYSIS AND TREATMENT

BY

PROF. W. O. ATWATER,

WESLEYAN UNIVERSITY, MIDDLETOWN, CONN.

BOSTON:
WRIGHT & POTTER PRINTING CO., STATE PRINTERS,
18 POST OFFICE SQUARE.
1886.

CONTENTS.

FOOD CONSUMPTION.

QUANTITIES, COSTS, AND NUTRIENTS OF FOOD-MATERIALS.

The food problem is one of the most important that can engross the attention of the people. It has a vital connection with the condition of the workingman, and the study of its various branches is essential to a proper understanding of the relative prosperity of industrial periods and the relative status of workingmen in different countries. It also has a directly practical interest for the wage worker, as it is undeniably true that much money is wasted in the purchase of food which is lacking in the elements of nutrition, and that the income of the working classes might be made far more effective if it were expended in accordance with the results of scientific research.

To supply in some measure the information necessary to enable the workingman to more intelligently regulate his expenditures for food, and thus enable him to secure with a given expenditure the maximum amount of nutritive elements, the Bureau has collected a number of schedules of dietaries, giving quantities and costs of food of people, mostly manual laborers, with limited incomes, in Massachusetts and Canada, which have been subjected to chemical analysis in order to estimate the quantities of nutritive material contained in them and to learn how they compare with regard to nutrients, cost, and fitness for their purpose with each other, as well as with other dietaries and with recognized standards.

It was not expected that either the data or the time at our disposal would suffice for exhaustive results, but rather that a brief preliminary study might be made which would serve to indicate the methods which should be followed, the sources of error and means for avoiding them, and the results which might be anticipated from a more detailed and complete inquiry, if such should at any time seem desirable and feasible. The results herewith presented are not brought forward as exhaustive therefore, but rather as a preliminary survey of a territory which promises rich rewards if thoroughly explored. While the data are to a certain extent incomplete, the final conclusions, it is believed, are not wide of the truth. The statistics of quantities of food, prices, etc., are compiled from original accounts with tradesmen, and may therefore be relied upon. The chief liability to error is undoubtedly to be found in the fact that the statistics give the amount of food purchased, not that actually eaten. Of the element of waste it is impossible to take accurate account. How much was wasted, or thrown away as refuse, cannot be ascertained. The housewives and boarding-house keepers would no doubt say that this element of waste was extremely small, and generally speaking this is no doubt true. Every effort has been made to eliminate error throughout the investigation, and it is not probable that the amount of error contained in the statistics is sufficient to affect materially the averages obtained.

GENERAL INTRODUCTION.

As the form in which the subject is here treated is, to most persons not specialists, somewhat new and a number of the technical terms employed, though common in late chemical and physiological treatises, have not yet worked their way into familiar use, it is proper to introduce here some general explanations, before proceeding to the discussion of the particular investigation undertaken by the Bureau.

A pound of lean beef (round steak freed from fat), and a quart of milk, both contain about the same quantity, say a quarter of a pound, of actually nutritive material. But the pound of beef costs more than the quart of milk and it is worth more as a part of a day's supply of food. The nutritive materials, or nutrients, as they are called, in the lean meat, though the same quantity as in the milk, are different in quality, and of greater nutritive value.

We have here an illustration of a fundamental fact in the economy of foods, namely, that the differences in the values of different foods depend upon both the kinds and the amounts of the nutritive material which they contain. If, then, we would understand the nutritive value of foods, we must know, first of all, what they are composed of. Knowing this, we must next consider what the several food ingredients do in the body; what is the special work which each one of the different nutrients has to perform in building up our bodies and in supplying their wants. When, in addition to all this, we know how much of each class of nutrients our bodies require and our food-materials contain we shall be in condition to economize our foods as we do the other necessaries of life.

The Nutrients of Food and their Uses in Nutrition.

Viewed from the standpoint of their uses in the nutrition of man, the constituents of ordinary foods may be succinctly classified as follows:

1. *Edible Substance:* the flesh of meats and fish; the shell contents of oysters; wheat flour.
2. *Refuse:* bones of meat and fish; the shells of oysters; bran of wheat.

The edible substance consists of

1. *Water.*
2. *Nutritive Substance, or Nutrients.*

Of the meat furnished by our butchers, the fish found in the market, and the other food for our tables, only a part serves to fulfil these purposes. The bone of roast beef is not used for food at all, and that of shad is worse than useless, because of the bother necessary to get rid of it; it is only the edible portion that is of actual value as food, the rest being merely refuse. And when we come to consider the edible portion, the meat freed from bone and gristle, the flesh of the fish, or the flour as it is baked in bread, we find that these consist largely of water. And although water is indispensable, that in the meat or the potatoes on our tables is of no more value for the support of our bodies than the same amount in milk or in a glass of water.

Leaving out of account, then, the refuse and the water, we have the nutritive materials, or, as we may call them, the nutrients of our foods. Speaking as chemists and physiologists, we may say that our food supplies, besides water, four principal classes of nutritive ingredients or nutrients, viz., protein, carbohydrates, fats, and mineral matters; and that these are transformed into the tissues and fluids of the body, muscle and fat, blood and bone, and are consumed to produce heat and force.

As this is not the place for detailed accounts of the nature and the uses of the constituents of foods, we can only recapitulate the main facts in tabular form, showing the principal nutrients of food, the composition of animal foods, and the constituents of vegetable foods and beverages.

PRINCIPAL NUTRIENTS OF FOODS.

Protein Compounds.*
- *Albuminoids or Proteids*: albumen of egg; myosin of muscle (lean of meat); casein of milk; gluten of wheat.
- *Gelatinoids*: ossein of bone; collagen of tendons (which boiled yield gelatin).

Fats: fats of meat; butter; olive oil; oil of maize and wheat.
Carbohydrates: starch; sugar; cellulose (woody fibre).
Mineral Matters, or Ash: calcium; potassium and sodium; phosphates and chlorides.

FUNCTIONS OF NUTRIENTS.

(Ways in which the nutrients are used in the body.)

The Protein of food
- forms the (nitrogenous) basis of blood, muscle, connective tissue, etc.
- is transformed into fats and carbohydrates.
- is consumed for fuel.

The Fats of food
- are stored as fat.
- are consumed for fuel.

The Carbohydrates of food
- are transformed into fat.
- are consumed for fuel.

---

* The muscular tissues of animals, and, hence, the lean portions of meat, fish, etc., contain small quantities of so-called nitrogenous extractives — creatin, carnin, etc. — which are the chief constituents of meat extract. These contribute materially to the flavor, and somewhat to the nutritive effect, of the foods containing them. They are not usually deemed of sufficient importance, however, to be grouped as a distinct class in tabular statements of the composition of foods. As they contain nitrogen, like the protein compounds, they are commonly included with the protein.

Perhaps a few words should be added regarding the principal classes of nutrients.

Protein, so called, " Flesh-formers," or " Flesh substance."— The terms protein, proteids, and albuminoids, are applied somewhat indiscriminately, in ordinary usage, to several or all of certain classes of compounds characterized by containing carbon, oxygen, hydrogen, and, with them, nitrogen. The most important are the proteids, or albuminoids, of which albumen, the white of egg, fibrin of blood, casein of milk, myosin (the basis of muscle), and gluten of wheat, are examples. Allied to these, but occurring in smaller proportions in animal tissues and foods, are the gelatinoids, the nitrogenous compounds that make the basis of connective and other tissues. Gelatin, whence the name gelatinoid (gelatin-like), is derived from some of these tissues, and may be taken as a type of the compound of this class. As these constituents are of similar constitution, and have similar, or nearly similar, uses in nutrition, it is customary to group them together as protein. What is especially to be borne in mind, then, is that protein is a term applied to the nitrogenous constituents of our foods, and we shall see these are, in general, the most important, as they are the most costly, of the nutrients.

Fats. — We have familiar examples of these in the fat of meat (tallow, lard), in the fat of milk, which makes butter, and in olive, cotton-seed, and other animal and vegetable oils. The fats consist of carbon, oxygen, and hydrogen, and contain no nitrogen. In nutritive value, as in cost, they rank next to the protein compounds. For some of the nutritive functions, indeed, namely, those expressed by the words " consumed for fuel," the fats greatly exceed protein in value.

Carbohydrates. — Starch, cellulose (woody fibre), sugar, and inosite ("muscle sugar"), and other similar substances, are called carbohydrates. Like the fats, they consist of carbon, oxygen, and hydrogen; but they have less carbon and hydrogen, and more oxygen than the fats, and hence taking weight for weight do not equal the fats in value for " fuel."

Mineral Matters, or Ash. — When vegetable or animal matters are burned, more or less incombustible material remains as ash. The ingredients which make the ash are called mineral matters, or, sometimes, salts. They are, for the most part, compounds of the elements, potassium, sodium, calcium and iron, with chlorine, sulphuric acid, and phosphoric acid. Sodium, combined with chlorine, forms sodium chloride, or common salt. Calcium, with phosphoric acid, forms calcium phosphate, or phosphate of lime, the mineral basis of bones.

Just how the different nutrients perform their different offices in nourishing the body, in building up its tissues, repairing its wastes, and serving as fuel to produce animal heat, and muscular and intellectual energy, is not yet fully known. Still, we have today a tolerably fair idea of the principal parts played by each class of nutrients.

Suppose that we have, for breakfast, beefsteak, bread and butter, and potatoes. The beef supplies us with considerable protein (in the lean meat) and fat. The butter is nearly all fat. The bread contains a little protein and fat. The potatoes the same ingredients, but in still smaller proportions, the principal nutrients of both bread and potatoes being starch, a carbohydrate.

Part of the protein of the food serves to repair the muscles, tendons, skin, and other organs, that are being worn out by constant use. The rest is consumed, sooner or later, — no one knows exactly when, where, or how. Part is probably transformed into fat, and stored as fat in the body, and thus replaces fat that is consumed to keep the body warm and to give the muscles strength for the work they have to do. And probably a part of the protein is changed into glycogen, a carbohydrate which occurs in the liver.

Part of the fat of the meat and bread is stored as fat in the body, and part is burned, yielding heat to keep the body warm, and muscular energy as well. The chief use of the carbohydrates, the starch and sugar, of the bread and potatoes seems to be to serve for fuel though they are transformed also into fats. It is a matter of common experience that many people are made corpulent by eating sugar and starchy foods, and grow lean when they avoid them.

The tables showing the composition of animal foods and the constituents of vegetable foods and beverages follow.

Composition of Animal Foods. Edible Portion — Flesh, etc., Freed from Bone, Shells, and other Refuse.

[Italics indicate European analyses, the rest are American.]

KINDS OF FOOD-MATERIALS.	Water.	Nutrients.	Protein (albuminoids).	Fats.	Carbohydrates.	Ash.
	Per cent.	Per cent.	Per cent.	Per cent.	Per cent.	Per cent.
MEATS — Fresh.						
Beef, side, well fattened, . .	54.7	45.3	17.2	27.1	–	1.0
Beef, lean, nearly free from fat,	76.0	24.0	21.3	0.9	–	1.3
Beef, round, rather lean, . .	66.7	33.3	23.0	9.0	–	1.3
Beef, sirloin, rather fat, . .	6.0 0	40.0	20.0	19.0	–	1.0
Beef, neck, ...	62.0	38.0	19.2	17.8	–	1.0
Beef, liver, ...	69.5	30.5	20.1	5.4	3.5	1.5
Beef, tongue, ...	63.5	36.5	17.4	18.0	–	1.1
Beef, heart, ...	56.5	43.5	16.3	26.2	–	1.0
Veal, lean, ...	78.8	21.2	19.7	0.8	–	0.7
Veal, rather fat, . . .	72.3	27.7	18.9	7.5	–	1.3
Mutton, side, well fattened, .	45.9	54.1	14.7	38.7	–	0.7
Mutton, leg, ...	61.8	38.2	18.3	19.0	–	0.9
Mutton, shoulder, . . .	58.6	41.4	18.1	22.4	–	0.9
Mutton, loin (chops), . .	49.3	50.7	15.0	35.0	–	0.7
MEATS — Prepared.						
Dried beef, ...	58.6	41.4	30.3	4.4	–	6.7
Corned beef, rather lean, . .	58.1	41.9	13.3	26.6	–	2.0
Smoked ham, ...	41.5	58.5	16.7	39.1	–	2.7
Pork, bacon, salted, . .	10.0	90.0	3.0	80.5	–	6.5
FOWL.						
Chicken, rather lean, . .	72.2	27.8	24.4	2.0	–	1.4
Turkey, medium fatness, .	66.2	33.8	23.8	8.7	–	1.3
Goose, fat, ...	38.0	62.0	15.9	45.6	–	0.5
DAIRY PRODUCTS, EGGS, ETC.						
Cow's milk, ...	87.4	12.6	3.4	3.7	4.8	0.7
Cow's milk, skimmed, . .	90.7	9.3	3.1	0.7	4.8	0.7
Cow's milk, buttermilk, .	90.3	9.7	4.1	0.9	4.0	0.7
Cow's milk, whey, . ..	93.2	6.8	0.9	0.2	5.0	0.7
Cheese, whole milk, . .	31.2	68.8	27.1	35.5	2.3	3.9
Cheese, skimmed milk, .	41.3	58.7	38.4	6.8	8.0	4.6
Butter, ...	9.0	91.0	1.0	87.5	0.5	2.0
Hen's eggs, ...	73.1	26.9	13.4	11.8	0.7	1.0
FISH, ETC.						
Flounder, whole, . .	84.2	15.8	13.8	0.7	–	1.3
Haddock, dressed, . .	81.4	18.6	17.1	0.3	–	1.2
Bluefish, dressed, . .	78.5	21.5	19.0	1.2	–	1.3
Cod, dressed, . . .	82.6	17.4	15.8	0.4	–	1.2
Whitefish, whole, . .	69.8	30.2	22.1	6.5	–	1.6
Shad, whole, . . .	70.6	29.4	18.5	9.5	–	1.4
Mackerel, average, whole, .	71.6	28.4	18.8	8.2	–	1.4
Salmon, whole, . . .	63.6	36.4	21.6	13.4	–	1.4
					⎰ Salt.	
Salt cod, ...	53.8	26.1	21.7	0.3	–	20.1	4.1
Smoked herring, . . .	34.5	53.8	36.4	15.8	–	11.7	1.6
Salt mackerel, . . .	42.2	47.2	22.1	22.6	–	10.6	2.5
Oysters, ...	87.2	12.8	6.0	1.2	3.6	2.0
Scallops, ...	80.3	19.7	14.7	0.2	3.4	1.4

Composition of Animal Foods. Specimens as Purchased in the Markets (including both Edible Portion and Refuse).

[Italics indicate European analyses, the rest are American.]

KINDS OF FOOD-MATERIALS.	Refuse: bones, skins, shells, etc.	EDIBLE PORTION.		NUTRIENTS.			
		Water.	Nutrients.	Protein (albuminoids).	Fats.	Carbohydrates, etc.	Mineral matters.
	Per cent.	Per cent.	Per cent.	Per cent.	Per cent.	Per cent.	Per cent.
MEATS — Fresh.							
Beef, side, well fattened, .	19.7	44.0	36.3	13.8	21.7	–	0.8
Beef, round, rather lean, .	10.0	60.0	30.0	20.7	8.1	–	1 2
Beef, sirloin, rather fat, .	25.0	45.0	30.0	15.0	14.3	–	0.7
Beef, neck, .	19.9	49.6	30.5	15.4	14.3	–	0.8
Beef, tongue, .	15.3	54.0	30.7	14.5	15.4	–	0.8
Beef, heart, .	6.0	53.4	40.6	14.8	24.8	–	1.0
Mutton, side, well fattened,	20.0	42.9	37.1	13.2	23.2	–	0.7
Mutton, leg, .	18.4	50.4	31.2	15.0	15.5	–	0.7
Mutton, shoulder, .	16.8	48.7	34.5	15.0	18.7	–	0.8
Mutton, loin (chops), .	16.3	41.3	42.4	12.5	29.3	–	0.6
MEATS — Prepared.							
Dried beef, .	6.5	55.5	38.0	27.4	4.2	–	6.4
Corned beef, rather lean, .	6.2	54.5	39.3	12.5	24.9	–	1.9
Smoked ham, .	12.5	36.3	51.2	14.6	34.2	–	2.4
Pork, bacon, salt, .	5.0	9.5	85.5	2.8	76.5	–	6.2
FOWL.							
Chicken, rather lean, .	41.6	42.2	16.2	14.2	1.2	–	0.8
Turkey, medium fatness, .	35.4	42.8	21.8	15.4	5.6	–	0 8
DAIRY PRODUCTS, EGGS, ETC.							
Cow's milk, .	–	87.4	12.6	3.4	3.7	4.8	0.7
Cow's milk, skimmed, .	–	90.7	9.3	3.1	0.7	4.8	0.7
Cow's milk, buttermilk, .	–	90.3	9.7	4.1	0.9	4.0	0.7
Cow's milk, whey, .	–	93.2	6.8	0.9	0.2	5.0	0.7
Cheese, whole milk, .	–	31.2	68.8	27.1	35.5	2.3	3.9
Cheese, skimmed milk, .	–	41.3	58.7	38.4	6.8	8.9	4.6
Butter, .	–	9.0	91.0	1.0	87.5	0.5	2.0
Hen's eggs, .	13.7	63.1	23.2	11.6	10.2	0.6	0.8
FISH, ETC.							
Flounder, whole,	66.8	27.2	6.0	5.2	0.3	–	0.5
Haddock, dressed, .	51.0	40.0	9.0	8.2	0.2	–	0.6
Bluefish, dressed, .	48.6	40.3	11.1	9.8	0.6	–	0.7
Cod, dressed, .	30.0	58.4	11.6	10.6	0.2	–	0.8
Whitefish, whole, .	53.5	32.5	14.0	10.3	3.0	–	0.7
Shad, whole, .	50.1	35.2	14.7	9.2	4.8	–	0 7
Mackerel, average, whole, .	44.6	40.4	15.0	10.0	4.3	–	0.7
Salmon, whole, .	35.3	40.6	24.1	14.3	8.8	–	1.0
Salt cod,	24.9	40.3	19.4	16.0	0.4	–	Salt 15.4 / 3.0
Smoked herring, .	44.4	19.2	29.9	20.2	8.8	–	6.5 / 0.0
Salt mackerel, .	33.3	28.1	31.5	14.7	15.1	–	7.1 / 1.7
Oysters, in shell, .	82.3	15.4	2.3	1.1	0.2	0.6	0.4
Oysters, solids, .	–	87.2	12.8	6.3	1.6	4.0	0.9
Scallops, edible portion, .	–	80.3	19.7	14.7	0.2	3.4	1.4

Constituents of Vegetable Foods and Beverages.

[The analyses of foods in Roman letters are American, those of foods and beverages in italics are European.]

KINDS OF FOOD AND BEVERAGES.	Water.	Protein (albuminoids).	Fats.	Carbohydrates, etc.	Woody fibre.	Mineral matters.
			NUTRIENTS.			
FOODS.	Per cent.	Per cent.	Per cent.	Per cent.	Per cent.	Per cent.
Wheat flour, average,*	11.6	11.1	1.1	75 4	0.2	0.6
Wheat flour, maximum,*	13.5	13.5	2.0	78.5	1.2	1.5
Wheat flour, minimum,*	8.3	8.6	0.6	68.3	0.1	0.3
Graham flour (wheat),	13.0	11.7	1.7	69.9	1.9	1.8
Cracked wheat,	10.4	11 9	1.7	74.6		1 4
Rye flour,	13.1	6.7	0 8	78.3	0.4	0.7
Pearled barley,	11 8	8.4	0.7	77.8	0.3	1.0
Buckwheat flour,	13.5	6.5	1.3	77.3	0.3	1.1
Buckwheat "farina,"	11.2	3.3	0.3	84.7	0.1	0.4
Buckwheat "groats,"	10.6	4.8	0.6	83.1	0.3	0.6
Oatmeal,	7.7	15.1	7 1	67.2	0.9	2.0
Maize meal,	14.5	9.1	3.8	69.2	1.8	1.6
Hominy,	13.5	8.3	0.4	77.1	0.3	0.4
Rice,	12.4	7.4	0.4	79.2	0.2	0.4
Beans,	13.7	23.2	2.1	53.7	3.7	3.6
Pease,	15.0	22.0	1.8	52.4	5.4	2.5
Potatoes,	75.5	2 0	0 2	20.5	0.8	1 0
Sweet potatoes,	75.8	1.5	0.4	20.0	1.1	1.2
Pole beans,	83.5	2.8	0.3	10.0	2.6	0.8
Green pease,	81.8	3.4	0.4	12 1	1.6	0.7
Turnips,	91 2	1.0	0¡2	6.0	0.9	0.7
Beets,	85.9	2.1	0.1	11.7	1.2	1.0
Carrots,	87.9	1 0	0.2	8.9	1.2	0.8
Onions,	89.3	1.1	0.2	8.3	0.6	0.5
Cabbage,	90.0	1.9	0.2	4.9	1.8	1 2
Lettuce,	94.3	1.4	0.3	2.2	0.7	1.1
Cauliflower,	90.4	2.5	0.4	5.0	0.9	0 8
Tomatoes,	92.4	1.3	0.3	4.6	0.8	0.6
Melons,	95.2	1.1	0.6	1.4	1.1	0.6
Pumpkins,	90.0	0.7	0.1	7.3	1.3	0.6
Squash,	87.8	0.7	0.2	9.1	1.1	1.1
Apples,	84.8	0 4	–	12.8	1 5	0.5
Pears,	83.0	0 4	–	12.0	4.3	0.3
Starch,	15.1	1.2	–	83.3	–	0.4
Tapioca,	13.3	0.6	86.0		–	0.1
Cane-sugar,	2.2	0.3	–	96.7	–	0 8
Molasses,	24.6	–	–	71.0	‡	2 3
Wheat bread,†	32.7	8.9	1 9	55.5		1.0
Graham bread,	34.2	9.5	1.4	53.3		1.6
Rye bread,	30.0	8.4	0.5	59.7		1 4
Soda crackers,	8 0	10.3	9.4	70.5		1.8
"Boston" crackers,	8.3	10 7	9.9	68.7		2.4
"Oyster" crackers,	3.9	12.3	4.8	76.5		2.5
Oatmeal crackers,	4.9	10.4	13.7	69.6		1.4
Pilot (bread) crackers,	7.9	12.4	4.4	74.2		1.1
Macaroni,	13.1	9.0	0.3	76.8		0.8
			Alcohol.		**Free acid.**	
BEVERAGES.						
Lager beer,	90.3	0.5	4.0	5.0	–	0.2
Porter and ale,	88.5	0.7	5.2	5.3	–	0.3
Rhenish wine, white,	86.3	–	10.5	2.6	0.4	0.2
Rhenish wine, red,	86.9	–	8.9	3.4	0.5	0.3
French wine, claret,	88.4	–	8 1	2.7	0 6	0.2

* Of analyses of American flours. The figures for "maximum" and "minimum" denote the largest and smallest percentages, respectively, found in the analyses. The sum of the figures representing the maximum must, therefore, exceed, and those for minimum fall below, 100 per cent.

† From flour of about average composition.   ‡ Other organic matter, 2.1.

Digestibility of Food-Materials as Affecting their Nutritive Values.

The question of the digestibility of foods is a very complex and difficult one, and it is to be noticed that the men who know the most about it are generally the least ready to make definite and sweeping statements as to the digestibility of this or that kind of food-material. One great difficulty is the fact that what we ordinarily call the digestibility of a food includes several different things, the ease with which it is digested, the time required for digesting it, and the proportions of its several constituents that are digested.

The ease of digestion of a given food-material and its suitableness to the digestive organs of a given person are physiological questions, hardly capable of categorical answer. The actual amounts digested are capable of more nearly accurate determination. Indeed, the percentage of the more important constituents of various foods actually digested by domesticated animals of different species, breeds, sexes, and ages, and under varying circumstances, has been a matter of active experimental investigation in the German agricultural experiment stations during the past twenty years. Briefly expressed, the method consists in weighing and analyzing both the food consumed and the solid excrement. Since the latter represents the amount of food undigested, the difference is the amount digested.

Such experiments upon human subjects, however, are rendered much more difficult by the necessity of avoiding complex mixtures of foods, in order that the digestibility of each particular food or food ingredient may be determined with certainty, and the fact that it is not easy to continue to eat the same kind of food long enough for a satisfactory experiment.

It is of course desirable to take account of the digestibility of food-materials in comparative statements of their nutritive values. The facts at hand are, however, hardly sufficient to warrant their introduction into food-tables. A considerable number of experiments have been carried out, nevertheless, the majority in the physiological laboratory of the University of Munich, Germany. The results of a number of them are concisely set forth in the following table :

Percentages of Undigested Matters in Food-Materials.

KIND OF FOOD EATEN.	Percentage of the dry food lost as excrement.	PERCENTAGES OF THE	
		Nitrogen* of the foods which goes to waste in the excrement.	Carbohydrates of the foods which go to waste in the excrement.
Lean beef,	5 or 6	2 or 3	–
Fish (haddock),	5 or 6	2 or 3	–
Eggs,	5¼	2½	–
Milk,	8 to 10	7 to 12	–
Milk, with cheese,	6 to 11	3 to 5	–
Rice,	4	2½	1
Potatoes,	9½	32	7½
Fat bacon, with some bread and beef,	6½ to 9½	12 to 14	2 to 6
White bread (wheat),	3¾ to 5¼	19 to 26	1 to 1¼
Coarse rye bread (black bread),	15	32	11
Cabbage,	15	18¼	15¼
Yellow beets,	21	39	18

* Protein.

Thus the men upon whom the experiments were made digested all but five or six per cent of the whole dry matter (water-free substance) of the lean beef and the fish, and all but two per cent of their protein (nitrogen). Of the water-free substance of milk, a somewhat larger proportion passed through the body undigested. The vegetable foods were much less completely digested, the coarse rye bread and the beets being, in this sense, the least digestible of all.

COSTS OF PROTEIN.

A subject that has received but little attention in this country, though it has become a vital one in Europe, and is becoming so with us, is the cost of the nutritive material of our foods. The relative cheapness or dearness of different foods must be judged by comparing, not the prices per pound, but the costs of the actual nutrients. In making such comparisons, the cost may be assumed to fall, not upon the inedible portions and the water, but solely upon the three classes of nutrients, the protein, fats, and carbohydrates. The relative physiological values of the nutrients in different foods depend upon (1) their digestibility and (2) their functions and the proportions in which they can replace each other in nutrition. An accurate physiological valuation is, in the present state of our knowledge, at least, impracticable. The pecuniary costs of the nutrients are, however, more nearly capable of approximation.

Various methods have been proposed for computing the relative pecuniary costs of the nutrients of foods, none of which, however, are entirely beyond criticism. The following, based upon German estimates of the relative costs of protein, fats, and carbohydrates, is perhaps as satisfactory as any. They are those of Prof. König.

From extended comparisons of the composition and market prices of the more important animal and vegetable food-materials, such as meats, fish, flour, etc., those which serve for nourishment and not as luxuries, and form the bulk of the food of the people, it has been estimated that a pound of protein costs, on the average, five times as much, and a pound of fats three times as much, as a pound of carbohydrates; that, in other words, these three classes of nutrients stand related to each other, in respect to cost, in the following proportions:

Assumed Ratios of Costs in Staple Foods.

Protein, ... 5
Fats, ... 3
Carbohydrates, ... 1

Perhaps a study of foods and prices in our markets might lead to a different scale of valuations, but this will serve our present purpose.

Suppose a pound of beef to cost 25 cents, and to contain 25 per cent of inedible matters, bone, etc., 45 per cent of water, and 30 per cent of nutritive substance, upon which latter — the bone and water being assumed to be without nutritive value — the whole cost comes. The 30 per cent, or $\frac{30}{100}$ pounds, of nutritive substance thus costs 25 cents, or at the rate of $83\frac{1}{3}$ cents per pound. If now we leave out of account the minute quantities of carbohydrates and the mineral matters, the whole cost will fall upon the protein and fats. Assuming these to cost in the ratio of $5:3$ and the amounts in the meat to be protein 15 per cent and fats $14\frac{1}{4}$ per cent, an easy computation will show the protein to cost 106 cents, and the fats 64 cents, per pound.*

---

* The methods of computing the cost of protein and the amounts obtained for 25 cents in different foods are shown in the foot-note on the next page.

Of the different nutrients, protein is physiologically the most important, as it is pecuniarily the most expensive. For these reasons the cost of protein in different food-materials may be used as a means of comparing their relative cheapness or dearness, as is done in the following table. The figures represent the ordinary prices per pound, and the corresponding costs of protein, in specimens of food-materials obtained in New York and Middletown, Conn., markets. Though the number of specimens is too small for reliable averages, the figures, taken together, doubtless give a tolerably fair idea of the relative costliness of the nutrients in the different classes of foods. It will be understood, of course, that the computations make allowance for the costs of the other nutrients, the fats and the carbohydrates, though for the sake of brevity the latter are omitted from the table.

---

1. *Cost of Protein :*—Suppose we wish to learn the costs of the nutrients in wheat flour, containing 11.1 per cent of protein, 1.1 per cent of fat, and 75.4 per cent of carbohydrates, and costing 4 cents a pound.

Let x represent the cost of a pound of carbohydrates in cents. Then, by the ratio of costs assumed above, a pound of fats would cost $3x$ cents and a pound of protein $5x$ cents. 100 pounds of the flour will cost 400 cents, and will contain 11.1 pounds of protein, 1.1 pounds of fats, and 75.4 pounds of carbohydrates. We shall have

$$75.4\,x \text{ cents} = \text{cost of } 75.4 \text{ pounds of carbohydrates.}$$
$$3.3\,x \text{ cents} = \text{"} \quad 1.1 \quad \text{"} \quad \text{fats.}$$
$$55.5\,x \text{ cents} = \text{"} \quad 11.1 \quad \text{"} \quad \text{protein.}$$

Total, . $134.2\,x$ cents $=$ " 100 " flour $=$ 400 cents.

Whence $x =$ 3 cents, cost of carbohydrates per pound.
$3x =$ 9 cents, " fats.
$5x =$ 15 cents, " protein.

2. *Amounts of Nutrients obtained for 25 cents :*—At 4 cents per pound for the flour, 25 cents will pay for 6.25 pounds. By the percentage composition above given 6.25 pounds of flour will contain 0.69 pound of protein, 0.07 pound of fats, and 4.71 pounds of carbohydrates, which are the amounts of nutrients obtained for 25 cents.

Comparative Cost of Protein in Food-Materials.

Food-Materials.	Prices per pound.	Cost of Protein per pound.	Food-Materials.	Prices per pound.	Cost of Protein per pound.
Meats.	Cents.	Cents.		Cents.	Cents.
Beef, sirloin,	25	106	Cod,	6	56
Mutton, leg,	22	91	Salt mackerel,	12.5	53
Beef, sirloin,	20	86	Salt cod,	7	43
Mutton, leg,	20	82	Mackerel,	5	40
Mutton, side,	20	73	Salt cod,	6	37
Beef, round,	18	70	Salt cod,	5	31
Mutton, leg,	16	66	Alewives,	3	27
Corned beef, lean,	18	60	Smoked herring,	6	24
Beef, round,	15	59			
Corned beef, lean,	15	55	*Dairy Products and Eggs.*		
Smoked ham,	18	51	Eggs, 40 cts. per dozen,	28	157
Smoked ham,	15	43	Eggs, 25 cts. per dozen,	18	101
Corned beef, lean,	10	36	Eggs, 15 cts. per dozen,	11	62
Beef, flank,*	15	36	Milk, 8 cts. per quart,	4	61
Beef, neck,	8	33	Milk, 7 cts. per quart,	3.5	53
Pork,* very fat, salted,	16	33	Cheese, whole milk,	19	37
Pork,* very fat, salted,	12	25	Cheese, whole milk,	13	27
Pork,* very fat, salted,	10	21	Cheese, skimmed milk,	8	18
Fish.			*Vegetable Foods.*		
Salmon,	100	511	Wheat bread,	8	38
Oysters, 50 cts. per quart,	25	336	Rice,	9	38
Oysters, 40 cts. per quart,	20	269	Potatoes,* $1.00 per bush.,	1.7	30
Oysters, 30 cts. per quart,	15	202	Wheat bread,	6	29
Lobsters,	12	202	Potatoes,* 75 cts. per bush.,	1.38	22
Salmon,	30	153	Wheat bread,	4	19
Flounder,	8	149	Beans, 13 cts. per quart,	6.5	18
Shad,	12	99	Wheat flour,	4.5	17
Bluefish,	10	98	Wheat flour,	4	15
Lake trout,	15	92	Oatmeal,	5	15
Halibut,	15	85	Beans, 10 cts. per quart,	5	14
Haddock,	7	84	Potatoes,* 50 cts. per bush.,	0.85	14
Mackerel,	10	79	Wheat flour,	3.5	13
Cod,	8	75	Corn meal,	3	12
Canned salmon,	20	70	Milk, 6 cts. per quart,	3	48
Shad,	8	66	Wheat flour,	3	12

* Containing little protein, the chief value being in other ingredients.

Thus the nutrients of vegetable foods are, in general, much less costly than in animal foods. The animal foods have, however, the advantage of containing a larger proportion of protein and fats, and the protein, at least, in more digestible forms.

Among the animal foods, those which rank as delicacies are the costliest. By the above calculations, the protein in the oysters costs from two to three dollars, and in salmon rises to over five dollars per pound. In beef, mutton, and ham it varies from 106 to 33 cents; in shad, bluefish, haddock, and halibut the range is about the same; while in cod and mackerel, fresh and salted, it varies from 75 to as low as 31 cents per pound. Salt cod and salt mackerel are nearly always, fresh cod and mackerel often, and even the choicer fish, as bluefish and shad, when abundant, cheaper sources of protein than any but the inferior kinds of meat. Among meats, pork is the cheapest; but salt pork or bacon has the disadvantage of containing very little protein.

It is well worth the noting that oatmeal is one of the cheapest foods that we have; that is, it furnishes more nutritive material, in proportion to the cost, than almost any other food. Corn meal is indeed cheaper, but the oatmeal has this great advantage over corn meal and wheat flour, that it has more protein. Of course, if we are to eat large quantities of lean meat — and many people, doubtless, eat more than is best for their health, saying nothing of their purses — the extra protein in the oatmeal is of little consequence to us. But if one wishes to economize in his food, oatmeal, rightly cooked, affords an excellent material therefor.

One of the most interesting things brought out in the table is the cheapness of the staple vegetable food-materials such as potatoes, wheat flour, corn meal, oatmeal, and beans.

AMOUNTS OF NUTRIENTS OBTAINED FOR 25 CENTS IN DIFFERENT FOOD-MATERIALS.

The above method of computing the relative expensiveness of different kinds of food-materials is, as has been said, open to the objection that it is based upon a certain assumed ratio of relative costs of protein, fats, and carbohydrates, which may or may not be right in any given case. A method free from these objections consists in computing how much of the several nutrients may be obtained for a given sum, for instance, 25 cents, in different food-materials. This is done in the following table:

Amounts of Nutrients Furnished for 25 Cents in Food-Materials at Ordinary Prices.

FOOD-MATERIALS.	Prices per Pound.	25 CENTS WILL PAY FOR—				
		Total Food-Material.	NUTRIENTS — POUNDS.			
			Total.	Protein.	Fats.	Carbo-hydrates.
Meats.	Cents.	Pounds.				
Beef, sirloin,	25	1.00	.29	.15	.14	-
Mutton, leg,	22	1.14	.34	.17	.17	-
Beef, sirloin,	20	1.25	.37	.19	.18	-
Mutton, leg,	20	1.25	.38	.19	.19	-
Beef, round,	18	1.39	.40	.29	.11	-
Mutton, side,	20	1.25	.46	.17	.20	-
Beef, round,	15	1.67	.49	.35	.14	-
Beef, neck,	8	3.13	.92	.48	.44	-
Pork, salted, fat,	16	1.56	1.23	.04	1.19	-
Pork, salted, fat,	12	2.08	1.65	.06	1.59	-
Pork, salted, fat,	10	2.50	1.98	.07	1.91	-
Fish.						
Salmon,	100	.25	.06	.04	.02	-
Oysters, 50 cts. per quart,	25	1.00	.12	.06	.02	.04
Oysters, 35 cts. per quart,	17.5	1.43	.17	.09	.02	.06
Salmon,	30	.83	.19	.12	.07	-
Bluefish,	10	2.50	.27	.25	.02	-
Shad,	12	2.08	.20	.19	.10	-
Cod,	8	3.13	.34	.33	.01	-
Mackerel,	10	2.50	.35	.25	.10	-
Canned salmon,	20	1.25	.44	.25	.19	-
Shad,	8	3.13	.44	.29	.15	-
Cod,	6	4.17	.45	.44	.01	-
Salt cod,	7	3.57	.58	.57	.01	-
Salt mackerel,	12.5	2.00	.60	.30	.30	-
Mackerel,	5	5.00	.71	.51	.20	-
Salt cod,	5	5.00	.82	.80	.02	-
Smoked herring,	6	4.17	1.21	.84	.37	-
Dairy Products and Eggs.						
Butter,	30	.83	.73	-	.73	-
Milk, 8 cts. per quart,	4	6.25	.74	.21	.23	.30
Milk, 7 cts. per quart,	3.5	7.14	.84	.24	.26	.34
Cheese, whole milk,	18	1.39	.90	.38	.49	.03
Milk, 6 cts. per quart,	3	8.33	.99	.28	.31	.40
Cheese, whole milk,	15	1.67	1.08	.45	.59	.04
Cheese, whole milk,	12	2.08	1.35	.56	.74	.05
Cheese, skim milk,	8	3.13	1.69	1.20	.21	.28
Vegetable Foods.						
Wheat bread,	8	3.13	2.08	.28	.06	1.74
Wheat bread,	6	4.17	2.75	.37	.07	2.31
Potatoes, $1.00 per bushel,	1.7	13.24*	3.04	.27	.03	2.74
Beans, 10 cts. per quart,	5	5.00	3.96	1.16	.11	2.69
Potatoes, 75 cts. per bushel,	1.25	18.00*	4.13	.36	.04	3.73
Wheat bread,	4	6.25	4.15	.56	.12	3.47
Oatmeal,	5	5.00	4.48	.76	.36	3.36
Wheat flour,	4.5	5.56	4.83	.62	.06	4.15
Wheat flour,	4	6.25	5.44	.60	.04	4.71
Wheat flour,	3.5	7.14	6.25	.79	.08	5.39
Potatoes, 50 cts. per bushel,	0.85	26.47*	6.06	.53	.05	5.48
Indian meal,	3	8.33	6.30	.70	.20	5.91
Wheat flour,	3	8.33	7.29	.02	.00	6.28

* The amounts for potatoes are actually, though not apparently, correct, allowance being made for waste, that is, adhering earth, etc.

We close this general introduction with the following table of consumption of food, etc., in a boarding-house, for thirty-nine weeks by 237 men, all laborers, presenting also the average weekly consumption per man for each article at a cost for each person of $1.30 per week. The table is compiled from original data secured by the Bureau.

Statistics of Boarding-House Consumption.

PERSONS.	Beans.	Beef.	But-ter.	Coffee.	Dried Apples.	Fish.	Flour.	Molas-ses.	Mut-ton.	Onions.
	bu.	lbs.	lbs.	lbs.	lbs.	lbs.	bbls.	gal.	lbs.	bu.
237 men, . . .	118	19,083	8,121	370	1,716	2,550	534	2,272	2,840	81
One man per week,	.012	2.12	.878	.04	.185	.275	.057	.245	.307	.008

Statistics of Boarding-House Consumption — Concluded.

PERSONS.	Pease.	Pork.	Pota-toes.	Rice.	Salt.	Soap.	Tea.	Tur-nips.	Vine-gar.	Milk.
	bu.	bbls.	bu.	bu	lbs.	lbs	lbs.	bu.	gals.	qts.
237 men, . . .	98	250	1,842	787	2,925	1,708	600	31	262	2,821
One man per week,	.01	.027	.199	.085	.316	.184	.064	.003	.028	.305

THE DIETARIES COLLECTED BY THE BUREAU.

The dietaries secured by the Bureau in the present investigation are for convenience divided into three series, designated as follows :

A. Miscellaneous, Massachusetts. These include fifteen dietaries of families and boarding-houses. The families are nearly all laboring people, while the boarders in the boarding-houses are mostly operatives in mills and factories, though some are clerks, dressmakers, etc. A few are French Canadians.

B. French Canadians, Massachusetts. These include nineteen dietaries of families and boarding-houses, all of French Canadians, the majority being operatives in mills and factories.

C. French Canadians, Canada. These include dietaries of twenty-seven families and boarding-houses in Montreal,

Quebec, and other places in Canada. The people are represented as all belonging to the laboring classes.

Series A and B are thus divided as the presence of French Canadian workers in Massachusetts affords an interesting opportunity for comparison, in regard to dietaries, of the same class of workers under the conditions surrounding them in their original habitations and Massachusetts, relatively. This opportunity did not present itself with respect to any other nationality which has selected Massachusetts as its home, and the results of the comparison will in a measure indicate the progress that has been made by the French Canadian since his emigration.

A number of representative dietaries have been selected from the total number collected in each series and subjected to detailed examination. The results are given under " Details of Dietaries."

The first object of the examination has been to learn the amounts of the principal nutrients — protein, fats, and carbohydrates — supplied in the several dietaries. To get them in uniform shape they have been transcribed to forms specially prepared for the purpose. These give :

First, a general statement of the number and classes of persons nourished by the dietary, with income and prices of board, where the prices are stated in the original reports.

Second, the amounts, cost, and estimated amounts of nutrients of the foods composing the dietary. The food-materials have been divided into (*a*) meats, fish, etc. ; (*b*) dairy products and eggs, and (*c*) vegetable food-materials.

Third, the estimates of the amounts, costs, and amounts of nutrients supplied per man per day. In a number of cases explanatory notes are added.

DATA UPON WHICH THE PRESENT STUDY OF DIETARIES
IS BASED.

The principal classes of data employed are the following :

Class A. Those contained in statistics of dietaries as collected and furnished for examination.

I. Statistics of food-materials.

    a. Kinds.
    b. Quantities.
    c. Costs.

II. Statistics of consumption of food-materials, that is, persons nourished and time.

    a. Number of persons nourished by food-materials.
    b. Sex   "   "   "   "   "
    c. Age   "   "   "   "   "
    d. Occupation   "   "   "   "
    e. Time during which the consumers were nourished.

Class B. Data obtained from other sources and used in the computations.

I. Chemical composition of the food-materials. Proportions of nutrients (nutritive ingredients) in each.

II. Relative nutritive effects of the several classes of nutrients, that is, proportions in which they may replace each other in the performance of certain functions of nutrition.

III. Proportions of nutrients required by persons of various classes, differing in age, sex, occupation, or other conditions by which the demand for nutrients is decided.

The statistics of Class A are set forth in the details of dietaries, and their principal facts presented in the tables on pages 305-310, *post.* The details of the dietaries are transcribed from the original schedules secured by the Bureau. The arrangement and classification of facts presented rest upon these dietaries.

The data of Class B demand somewhat more detailed explanations and comments, which we now present.

COMPOSITION OF FOOD-MATERIALS.

A large number of analyses of meats, vegetables, and other food-materials have been made in Europe, but only comparatively few analyses of American food-materials other than cereal and dairy products have been reported. A number of specimens, — some three hundred — mostly of fish and meats, but some of other food-materials, have, however, been analyzed at the instance of the United States Fish Commission

and National Museum, but await publication. These latter
have been used, with other available data from home and
foreign sources, for the present calculation. As may be seen
in the explanatory notes accompanying the details of dietaries,
there are for a few materials no analyses available. For these
cases, fortunately few and of relatively small importance,
estimates have been made.

All our ordinary food-materials vary more or less in composition, and wherever the specimens actually used cannot be
analyzed, averages of analyses of other specimens must be used
as estimates. For most vegetable foods and dairy products the
range of variation is not so wide but that, with the number of
analyses at hand, such averages will serve tolerably well. The
same may be said of most of our common species of food fishes.
But with meats the case is somewhat different, since there are
wide variations, not only in the composition of meat from animals
of different kinds, but in that from different animals of the same
kind and in that from different parts of the same animal.

The method of estimating the composition of beef was as
follows:

Among the analyses above referred to as executed in behalf
of the National Museum were those of a series of specimens of
beef. A large amount, the larger part, we are informed, of
the beef consumed in many of our Eastern cities is so-called
" Chicago " or " Western " beef, which is slaughtered in Chicago or elsewhere and brought East. From a carload of
" Chicago beef" a side was selected by an experienced
dealer as of average quality, especial pains being taken to
secure one of average fatness.

This side of beef was divided into twenty-five pieces, or
" cuts," in the manner common in New York markets, and
portions of each piece, sufficient to represent the whole, were
analyzed, the proportions of refuse (bone, gristle, etc.),
water, and nutrients being determined.

A diagram representing these divisions of the beef was placed ·
in the hands of the collectors of the dietaries here examined, who,
so far as practicable, indicated in their statements the parts of the
animal from which the beef of the several dietaries was taken.
The manner of cutting up the beef differs in different places, but
not sufficiently to very materially affect the estimates. A more

serious matter is the variation of different specimens of beef and it is, of course, a question whether the side selected for analysis, as above stated, fairly represents the average of the kinds in the dietaries. We are informed that in all the Massachusetts cities, where the dietaries were collected, nearly all the beef used is so-called "Chicago beef," and it is probable that the analyses fairly indicate the quality of the beef sold.

As the best way for utilizing these data an assistant has gone over the dietaries, noted the "cuts" of beef where stated and ascribed to each the percentages of nutrients found in the analyses of corresponding "cuts." The results are shown in the following table. Where the original includes two or more "cuts" in one entry the average is taken. The several computations for "roast beef" are averaged together. The same is done for "beef stew," "beef steak," etc., and some of these latter averages are incorporated in the table on pages 261 and 262, giving the percentages of nutrients in food-materials assumed in analyses of dietaries.

Composition of Different Parts of Beef.

Current number of dietary.	Portion ("Cut") of Beef.	Protein.	Fat.
		Per cent.	Per cent.
A 7	Beef, hip sirloin, ...	12.5	10.6
A 7 and B 6	Beef, brisket, shoulder clod, and cross ribs, . . .	13.9	25.9
A 7	Beef, socket and rump, ...	11.5	26.6
A 7	Beef, second cut, chuck ribs, ...	16.3	16.2
A 7	Beef, ribs, ...	11.9	28.3
B 1	Beef, top of sirloin and second cut of round, . .	13.4	24.0
B 4	Beef, top of sirloin, ...	12.9	42.1
B 5	Beef, plate, navel, and second cut of ribs, . .	12.4	30.6
B 10	Beef, shoulder clod, cross ribs, and top of sirloin, .	14.1	29.4
B 12	Beef, rump, ...	12.2	37.0
B 13	Beef, plate and second cut ribs, ...	11.9	29.9
A 5	Roast beef, first cut, round, ...	17.9	12.3
A 8	Roast beef, second cut ribs, and third cut ribs, . .	11.6	27.9
A 10	Roast beef, shoulder clod and cross ribs, . . .	14.6	23.0
A 13	Roast beef, second cut, chuck ribs, ...	16.3	16.2
	Roast beef, average, ...	15.1	19.9
A 4	Beef, roast and boiled, chuck ribs, ...	15.4	17.6
A 2	Beef steak, round, ...	16.8	10.6
A 4	Beef steak, first cut, chuck ribs, ...	13.7	23.0
A 5 and A 13	Beef steak, first cut, round, ...	17.9	12.3
A 8, A 9, A 11, and A 12	Beef steak, hip sirloin, ...	12.5	16.6
	Beef steak, average, ...	14.5	15.6
A 1 and A 2	Beef stew, shoulder clod and flank, ...	14.0	31.3
A 4	Beef, corned, brisket, plate, and top of sirloin, . .	11.4	31.9
A 5	Beef, corned, brisket, cross ribs, plate, and shoulder clod,	12.2	24.7
A 13	Beef, corned, brisket and plate, ...	11.3	28.8
A 9 and A 10	Beef, corned, brisket, ...	11.2	28.6

The figures used in calculating the amounts of nutrients in the dietaries are generally given in the table showing the percentages of nutrients in food-materials assumed in analyses of dietaries. In some special cases, however, they are not given in this table but are stated with explanations in the explanatory notes appended to the details of the dietaries in which they are used.

To insure perfect accuracy it would, of course, be necessary to analyze the materials actually used in each case. It is probable that while divergences, in some cases very wide, might occur, the figures for the composition of each dietary, as a whole, would be substantially accurate.

The item about which there seems to be the most question is the quantity of fat in the meats, especially the beef. The analyses here used accord very closely with European figures for very fat beef.* Numerous observations, however, which cannot be detailed here but which seem to be but little short of decisive, imply that the beef commonly used on the continent of Europe is, on the average, less fat than the average beef in our markets. It is certain that much of that commonly used in our Eastern cities is very much fatter than that here analyzed and taken as the bases of these computations.

Attention has been called elsewhere to the fact that the figures for weights of food-materials in the dietaries represent the quantities purchased and do not indicate how much was eaten. The rejection of a considerable part of the fat of meats by many persons is one of the most common of dietary facts, at least in the Northern and Eastern States. Some of the fat of beef is left with the butcher, much goes to the soap maker and much more into the garbage. But a surprisingly large part of the fat of our beef is so diffused through the lean, much of it in invisible particles, that when we have cut out the larger pieces of fat from our roast beef or our steak and left them on our plates, we, nevertheless, eat the bulk of the actual fat of the meat with the lean and the small portions of visible fat which adhere to it.

Especial stress is laid on this point because the dietaries here studied indicate a remarkably large consumption of fat in this country. The possible bearing of this fact upon our national dietetics may be extremely important.

---

* König Nahrungsmittel, second edition, volume I., page 5.

Percentages of Nutrients in Food-Materials Assumed in Analyses of Dietaries.

[The figures of this table have been employed for estimating the amounts of nutrients in the dietaries, except in such cases as are hereinafter mentioned.]

FOOD-MATERIALS.	Protein.	Fats.	Carbohydrates.
	Per cent.	Per cent.	Per cent.
Meat, Fish, etc.			
Beef,*	13.5	25.0	–
Beef, roast,*	15.1	19.9	–
Beef, roast and boiled,* . . .	15.4	17.6	–
Beef steak,*	14.5	15.6	–
Beef stew,*	14.0	31.3	–
Beef, corned,*	11.5	28.5	–
Beef, tongue, ...	14.8	15.3	–
Beef, liver, ...	20.0	5.4	3.5
Beef, tripe,*	21.0	1.0	–
Veal,*	15.2	5.6	–
Mutton, ...	13.9	23.5	–
Mutton, fore-quarter, . . .	13.6	23.8	–
Mutton, hind-quarter, . . .	14.2	23.1	–
Mutton, leg, ...	15.0	15.5	–
Mutton chop, ...	14.2	23.1	–
Pork, roast, ...	11.4	36.2	–
Pork steak, ...	11.4	36.2	–
Pork, ham, ...	14.6	34.3	–
Pork, sausage, ...	13.2	39.1	–
Pork, salt, ...	2.8	76.5	–
Pork, corned, ...	10.7	39.7	–
Lard, ...	–	99.0	–
Fowl (chicken), ...	14.3	1.2	–
Cod, ...	11.0	0.3	–
Haddock, ...	8.3	0.1	–
Cod and haddock, . . .	9.7)	0.2	–
Mackerel, ...	10.1	3.9	–
Halibut, ...	15.1	4.2	–
Salt cod, ...	16.0	0.4	–
Salt mackerel, . . .	14.7	15.1	–
Eggs and Dairy Products.			
Eggs, ...	11.6	10.2	0.6
Milk, ...	3.4	3.7	4.8
Cheese, ... ' .	27.1	35.5	2.3
Butter, ...	1.0	87.5	0.5
Vegetable Foods.			
Wheat flour, ...	11.1	1.1	75.4
Graham flour, ...	11.7	1.7	69.9
Rye flour, ...	6.7	0.8	78.3
Barley, ...	8.4	0.7	77.8
Oatmeal, ...	15.1	7.1	67.2
Corn meal, ...	9.1	3.8	69.2
Tapioca, ...	0.6	–	86.0
Rice, ...	7.4	0.4	79.2
Beans, ...	23.2	2.1	53.7
Pease, ...	22.9	1.8	52.4
Potatoes,*	1.9	0.2	18.4
Turnips,*	0.9	0.2	(5.1
Carrots,*	0.9	0.2	7.6
Cabbage,*	1.7	0.2	4.4
Cauliflower,*	2.0	0.3	4.0
Squash,*	0.5	0.1	5.3
Onions,*	1.0	0.2	7.5
Lettuce, ...	1.4	0.3	2.2
Beets,*	1.8	0.1	10.0
Green pease, ...	3.4	0.4	12.1 '
Pole beans (green), . . .	2.8	0.3	10.0
Green corn,*	4.6 –	1.9	34.6
Tomatoes, ...	1.3	0.3	4.5
Apples,*	0.3	–	10.9
Cranberries,*	0.5	–	8.4
Corn starch,*	–	–	83.3

* These analyses are estimated from such data as are available. Those for beef have been previously explained (see table on page 259). Those for veal and for vegetable foods are computed from standard analyses by making allowance for assumed proportions of waste.

Percentages of Nutrients in Food-Materials, etc. — Concluded.

Food-Materials.	Protein.	Fats.	Carbohydrates.
	Per cent.	Per cent.	Per cent.
Sugar, ...	-	-	96.7
Molasses, ...	-	-	71.0
Syrup, ...	-	-	71.0
Raisins, ...	2.5	0.6	63.0
Dried currants, ...	2.5	0.6	63.0
Wheat bread, ...	8.9	1.9	55.5
Boston crackers, ...	10.7	9.9	68.7
Soda crackers, ...	10.3	9.4	70.5
Oyster crackers, ...	12.3	4.8	76.5

STANDARDS FOR DAILY DIETARIES.

The ordinarily accepted standards for dietaries are estimated in terms of the three most important classes of nutritive ingredients, or nutrients, of foods, namely, protein (or albuminoids), fats, and carbohydrates. The amounts of these appropriate for daily rations for different classes of people under different conditions have been estimated in two ways :

1. By observing the amounts actually consumed by people whose circumstances of life would permit reasonably good nourishment and at the same time preclude any considerable waste of food.

2. By direct experiments, in which the income and outgo of the body are directly compared. Our best information on this subject comes from Germany where studies have been made by numerous investigators, including Liebig, Moleschott, Ranke, Forster, and especially Voit. Payen, in France, and Frankland, Playfair, Lawes, and Gilbert, in England, have also made most valuable contributions to the knowledge of this subject.

The fact deserves mention, however, that very little attention appears to have been paid to the results of the latest and best research in this direction. Even the text-books in chemistry and physiology, which are looked upon as most authoritative, are too apt to pass the subject over most superficially or almost ignore it.

Rations Estimated from Dietaries. Perhaps the best way of illustrating the amounts of nutrients estimated to be actually consumed by different persons will be to give some examples. The following will serve the purpose. The weights are, for convenience, given in grams. It will be remembered that about 454 grams equal a pound and 28.4 grams, an ounce, avoirdupois.

Nutrients in Daily Dietaries.

DESCRIPTION.	Protein: total.	Protein: digesti-ble.	Fats.	Carbo-hydrates.
A. *Poorly nourished.*	Grams.	Grams.	Grams.	Grams.
1 Sewing girl, London, England : 1863. Wages, 93 cts. per week.	53	40	33	315
2 Weaver, Coventry, England.	60	43	28	398
3 Agricultural laborer, England.	96	73	48	517
4 Agricultural laborer, Ireland.	92	69	42	519
5 Agricultural laborer, Silesia; mostly vegetable food.	80	–	16	552
6 Seamstress, Leipsic, Germany.	56	47	50	229
7 Laborer, Leipsic, Germany.	–	56	37	290
8 Laborer, Hildesheim, Germany; diet mostly potatoes.	86	–	13	610
9 Monk in cloister; diet of bread, beer, soup, and vege-tables.	68	–	11	469
B. *Well nourished.*				
10 " Well-fed " tailor, England.	131	–	39	524
11 Weaver, at hard work, England.	151	–	43	621
12 Blacksmith, England.	176	–	71	666
13 Prize fighter, England; diet mostly meat.	288	–	88	93
14 Average for adults, moderate exercise, England (Play-fair's estimate).	120	–	40	530
15 Average for hard working laborer, England (Play-fair's estimate).	160	–	66	579
16 Mechanic, 60 years old, Munich, Germany.	117	–	68	345
17 Serving man, 36 years old, Munich, Germany.	133	–	95	422
18 Mechanic, 40 years old, Munich, Germany.	131	–	63	464
19 Well paid mechanic, Munich, Germany.	151	–	54	479
20 Physician, Munich, Germany.	134	–	102	291
21 University professor, Munich, Germany; very little muscular exercise.	100	–	100	220
22 Privy Councillor, Marburg, Germany; very little mus-cular exercise.	90	–	79	285
23 Brewery laborer, Munich, Germany; severe labor.	190	–	73	600
24 Lumberman, Bavaria; diet of fat and flour (bread).	112	–	309	691
25 German soldier, peace footing.	117	–	26	547
26 German soldier, war footing.	151	–	46	522
27 German soldier, war footing, extraordinary ration.	191	–	63	607

Numbers 1 to 8 represent quantities of food consumed by very poor people and are not adequate for healthful nourish-ment. That of the seamstresses may be regarded as barely sufficient to sustain life. All these, it will be noticed, are especially deficient in protein.

Number 9, that of a monk in a cloister, whose habits were such as to involve little muscular or other exertion, was, doubtless, not so far short of the needs of the body.

All the rest, those of moderately and well-fed persons, except numbers 21 and 22, contain more protein and usually more fat. In general, the larger the income or the more severe the labor the greater is the consumption of protein. The variations are, however, very wide and individual excep-tions numerous. Note, for instance, the English prize fighter, with his diet of meat, and the Bavarian lumberman, who has little else than bread and fat.   Their dietaries furnish daily :

DESCRIPTION.	Protein.	Fats.	Carbohydrates.
	Grams.	Grams.	Grams.
Prize fighter, ...	288	88	93
Lumberman, ...	112	309	691

These are extreme, and indeed abnormal, cases. The majority approach reasonably near to each other, as may be observed in numbers 10, 14, 16, 17, 18, 19, and 25, which are rations of ordinary men with moderate muscular exercise, and numbers 11, 12, 15, 23, and 26, which are those of persons of whom severe labor is required. Numbers 21 and 22 have smaller amounts of protein, but they are dietaries of persons with presumably little muscular exercise. Number 27, on the other hand, which is very heavy in protein, is a ration for a soldier in extra hard marching and fighting.

Direct Experiments in which the Income and the Outgo of the Body are Compared. Experiments of this sort are made by supplying individuals with food of known amount and composition and determining the quantity and composition of the products given off from the body. The most interesting and valuable researches of this class are those with the respiration apparatus. This permits the keeping of an accurate account of all the items of income and outgo, the food, drink, and inhaled air, which make up the former, and the solid and liquid excreta and exhaled air, which make up the latter, being measured, weighed, and analyzed. The experiments involve an immense amount of labor but bring correspondingly complete and reliable results. A discussion of them here would, however, be out of place.

It is sufficient to say that from the data obtained from the two sources named, the estimates of composition of dietaries and the direct experiments, various standards for daily rations have been computed. The standard rations assumed by Prof. Voit and the Munich school of physiological chemists are more commonly accepted than any others, and are most frequently followed in estimating dietaries. The following are examples :

Standards for Daily Dietaries.

CLASSIFICATION.	Protein.	Fats.	Carbohydrates.
	Grams.	Grams.	Grams.
Children to 1½ years, ...	20 to 36	30 to 45	60 to 90
Children from 6 to 15 years, . . .	70 to 80	37 to 50	250 to 400
Laboring man at moderate work, . .	118	56	500
Laboring man at severe work, . . .	145	100	450
Laboring woman, ...	92	44	400
Aged man, ...	100	68	350
Aged woman, ...	80	50	260

We are, of course, to understand that these figures represent only general averages. It is assumed that for an ordinary laboring man, doing an ordinary amount of work, the amounts of nutrients above stated will suffice, that with them he will hold his own, and that any considerable excess above these quantities will be superfluous. Of course, no one expects any given man to adjust his diet exactly to this standard. He may need more, and may perhaps get on with less. He may eat more fats and less carbohydrates, or he may consume more protein, if he is willing to pay for it. If, however, he has much less protein, and keeps up his muscular exertion, he will be apt, sooner or later, to suffer.

Of course different individuals, though subjected to like conditions, will both require and consume different quantities of nutrients. In general the larger the person, that is, the more bulk of machinery there is in the organism, the more of protein and other nutrients will be consumed. Hence men need on the average more than women and children. The requirements vary with the muscular activity. A man at hard work requires more of protein and of other nutrients than one at lighter work or rest. Aged people, who are generally less active than those in the prime of life, require less food and less protein. But we shall probably not go very far amiss in adopting these standards. One point, however, demands special consideration.

ESTIMATES OF COMPARATIVE QUANTITIES OF NUTRIENTS REQUIRED BY PERSONS OF DIFFERENT CLASSES.

Since the people nourished by the dietaries here examined differ in age, sex, and occupation, and hence differ likewise in their demands for nutriment, and since a chief object of the examination is to compare the dietaries with one another in respect to the quantities of actual nutrients supplied, it is clear that to attain our object we need some standard for estimating the relative demands of people of different classes. If, for instance, we could take a particular class, as laboring men at moderate work, and find to how many average men of this class the people nourished by each dietary would be equivalent in their demands for nutrients, we should simply have to divide the total quantity of nutrients supplied per day by this equivalent number of men to get the quantities per man per day. The results thus obtained for the several dietaries would, when compared with each other and with accepted standards, give us what we seek.

We are of the opinion that the experimental data on record in European works, if rightly collated and worked up, would give a basis for at least an approximate estimate of the comparative requirements of the several classes of persons into which those nourished by the food of these dietaries would most properly be divided. Indeed, the figures cited in the table of standards for daily dietaries will help in arriving at such a basis. Thus we have:

Quantities of Nutrients Appropriate for Daily Dietaries.

PERSONS.	Protein.	Fats.	Carbohydrates.
	Grams.	Grams.	Grams.
Children to 1½ years old, ...	28	37	75
Children, 6 to 15 years old, ...	75	43	325
Woman at ordinary work, ...	92	44	400
Laboring man at moderate work, . . .	118	56	500

Late research has thrown considerable light upon equivalent values of these three classes of nutrients for at least a part of their work in the body. The proportions in which they replace each other in the performance of functions they have in common, as indicated by experiments with animals in the respiration apparatus, in Munich, agree almost exactly with the figures representing their quantities of potential energy as shown by burning the same materials in the calorimeter. On the basis of extended experiments of both the kinds named it has been estimated[*] that the average amounts of potential energy in the three principal classes of nutrients are, approximately :

In 1 gram of protein, ... 4.1 calories
" " " " fats, ... 9.3 "
" " " " carbohydrates, . . . 4.1 "

On this basis the potential energy in the nutrients of the dietaries assumed as standards would be :

Children to 1½ years, ... 767 calories
Children, 6 to 15 years, ... 2,041 "
Woman at ordinary work, . . . 2.426 "
Laboring man at moderate work, . . 3,055 "

These figures are in about the following relative proportions. We interpolate an assumed value for children from 6 to 2 years of age.

Estimated Relative Quantities of Potential Energy in Nutrients required by Persons of Different Classes.

Laboring man at moderate work, ... 10
Woman at ordinary work, ... 8
Child, 15 to 6 years old, ... 7
Child, 6 to 2 years old, ... 5
Child, under 2 years old, ... 2½

The application of these figures is simple. The food of dietary A1, for instance, suffices for 77 persons (factory operatives), 66 males and 11 females. The figures allot to one working woman 0.8 as much nutritive material as to one laboring man at moderate work. This would make the 11 women equivalent to (8.8) 9 men, which added to 66 would make the whole 77 persons equal to 75 men. The 77 persons during 30 days, the time covered by the dietary, would be equal in requirements to one man for 2,250 days. The estimates in the dietaries hereinafter presented are made in this way.

DETAILS OF DIETARIES.

The tables on pages 269–305, as previously stated, contain details of a number of dietaries selected from a much larger number collected by the Bureau in the early Fall of last year. Besides the fifteen dietaries, five for each series, for which the details are used in the analyses tables on pages 305–310, *post*, the remaining dietaries here given in detail have been also examined and the quantities of nutrients determined, but the results are included only in the averages contained in the analyses tables. The numbers are as follows:

CLASSIFICATION.	A. Miscellaneous, Massachusetts.	B. French Canadian, Massachusetts.	C. French Canadian, Canada.
Given in detail, and used in the analyses tables, ...	5	5	5
Given in detail, but included in the averages only, ...	5*	2*	8
Not used, ...	5	12	14
Totals, ...	15	19	27

* Series A included three French Canadian dietaries which are averaged with those of series B, making 10 of the latter, all told, in the averages of series B in the tables on pages 306–310.

Some of the quantities of nutrients have been calculated from measures to weights in accordance with the following tabular statement. A few minor alterations and additions are explained in the notes appended to the several tables of dietaries. Otherwise no material changes other than those of form of statement have been introduced in transcribing.

Equivalent Measures and Weights.

ARTICLES.	Basis.	Equivalent in Weight.	
		Lbs.	Ozs.
Potatoes, beets, turnips, and tomatoes, . . .	bushel	60	–
Beans* and pease, ...	bushel	60	–
Beans and pease, ...	quart	1	14
Apples, ...	barrel	150	–
Onions, ...	bushel	52	–
Molasses, ...	gallon	11	–
Syrup, ...	gallon	12	–
Milk, ...	quart	2	–
Eggs,†	dozen	1	6

* 60–62 lbs.

† In Canada, 1 lb. 8 oz. per dozen.

Series A.   Miscellaneous, Massachusetts.

The five dietaries of this series which are given in detail and used in the analyses tables include three of boarding-houses and two of families in Lowell, Lynn, East Cambridge, and Boston.   Two more of boarding-houses, one in Lowell and one in Lawrence, are also given in detail, but the results are included only in the averages, for this series, in the analyses tables.   The results for three dietaries of French Canadian families in North Cambridge, of this series, are also included in the averages for series B in the analyses tables.   The persons are factory and mill operatives, mechanics, etc., with a few clerks and dressmakers.   With these statements and the explanatory notes accompanying the several schedules, further explanations will not be needed.

DIETARY NUMBER, A 1.

Description: Boarding-house in Lowell, Mass., of 77 persons, 66 males and 11 females. Boarders, mill operatives. Time, one month. Estimated as equivalent in demands for nutrients to 75 laboring men at moderate work for 30 days, or 1 man for 2,250 days.

ANALYSIS.

Kinds.	Prices per lb.	Quanti- ties.	Costs.	Protein.	Fats.	Carbohy- drates.
	cents.	lbs.		lbs.	lbs.	lbs.
Beef, roast,	10	400	$40 00	60.4	79.9	–
Beef steak,	14	272	38 08	39.4	42.4	–
Beef, corned,	7	350	24 50	40.3	99.3	–
Beef tongue,	10	62	6 20	9.2	9.5	–
Beef stew,	5	167	8 35	23.4	52.3	–
Beef, tripe,	6	20	1 20	4.2	0.2	–
Pork, roast,	10	150	15 00	17.1	54.3	–
Ham,	11	160	17 60	23.4	54.9	–
Salt pork,	10	70	7 00	2.0	53.6	–
Lard,	8	260	20 80	–	257.4	–
Haddock,	7	168	11 76	13.9	0.2	–
Halibut,	12	50	6 00	7.6	2.1	–
Mackerel,	3	40	1 20	4.0	1.6	–
Salt fish (cod),	4½	50	2 25	8.0	0.2	–
Total meats, fish, etc.,		2,219	$199 94	252.9	708.4	–
Milk,	2	3,024	$60 48	102.8	111.9	145.2
Cheese,	11	63.5	6 98	17.2	22.5	1.5
Butter,	22 and 10	291	54 54	2.9	254.6	1.5
Eggs,	14	107	14 82	12.4	10.9	0.6
Total dairy products and eggs,		3,485.5	$136 82	135.3	399.9	148.8
Flour,	3	1,568	$47 04	174.0	17.2	1,182.3
Sugar,	7½	600	45 00	–	–	580.2
Molasses,	4½	99	4 50	–	–	70.3
Beans,	3	124	3 74	28.8	2.6	66.6
Rice,	8	25	2 00	1.9	0.1	19.9
Oatmeal,	4	25	1 00	3.8	1.9	16.3
Potatoes,	1	2,520	25 20	47.9	5.0	463.7
Squash,	1½	250	3 75	1.3	0.3	13.3
Onions,	2	26	50	0.3	–	2.0
Beets,	5-9	90	50	1.6	0.1	9.0
Turnips,	5-6	120	1 00	1.1	0.2	6.1
Tomatoes,	5-6	120	1 00	1.0	0.4	5.4
Apples,	1⅔	300	5 00	0.9	–	32.7
Raisins,	12½	24	3 00	0.6	0.1	15.1
Currants,	10	15	1 50	0.3	–	9.5
Corn starch,	9	12	1 08	–	–	11.0
Crackers,	5	48	2 40	5.1	4.8	34.0
Total vegetable food,		5,966	$148 21	269.2	32.6	2,537.9
Total animal food,		5,704.5	336 76	388.2	1,108.3	148.8
Total food,		11,670.5	$484 97	657.4	1,140.9	2,686.7
Meats, fish, etc., per man per day,		.99	$0 09	.11	.31	–
Dairy products and eggs, per man per day,		1.55	06	.06	.18	.07
Animal food per man per day,		2.54	$0 15	.17	.49	.07
Vegetable food, " "		2.65	07	.12	.01	1.13
Total food, " "		5.19	$0 22	.29	.50	1.20

Dietary Number, A 2.

Description : Boarding-house in Lowell, Mass., of 70 persons, 10 males and 60 females. Boarders, mill operatives. Time, one month. Estimated as equivalent in demands for nutrients to 58 men for 30 days, or 1 man for 1,740 days.

ANALYSIS.

Kinds.	Prices per lb.	Quantities.	Costs.	Protein.	Fats.	Carbohydrates.
	cents.	lbs.		lbs.	lbs.	lbs.
Beef, ...	10	425	$42 50	57.4	106.3	–
Beef steak, ...	16	250	40 00	36.3	39.0	–
Beef, corned, . . .	7	300	21 00	34.5	85.5	–
Beef stew, . .	5	100	5 00	14.0	31.3	–
Pork, roast, ...	10	100	10 00	11.4	36.2	–
Ham, ...	12	150	18 00	21.9	51.5	–
Salt pork, ...	10	25	2 50	0.7	19.1	–
Lard, ...	8	150	12 00	–	148.5	–
Cod and haddock, . .	7	150	10 50	14.6	0.3	–
Halibut, ...	14	50	7 00	7.6	2.1	–
Total meats, fish, etc., . .		1,700	$168 50	198.4	519.8	–
Butter, ...	20	150	$30 00	1.5	131.3	0.7
Cheese, ...	10	30	3 00	8.1	10.7	0.7
Milk, ...	2	2,000	40 00	68.0	74.0	96.0
Eggs, ...	16	69	11 00	8.0	7.0	0.4
Total dairy products and eggs, ...		2,249	$84 00	85.6	223.0	97.8
Flour, ...	3¼	1,372	$44 59	152.3	15.1	1,034.5
Rice, ...	8	15	1 20	1.1	–	11.9
Corn starch, . . .	9	10	90	–	–	8.3
Crackers, ...	5	48	2 40	5.1	4.8	33.0
Sugar, ...	7	400	28 00	–	–	386.8
Molasses, ...	4½	77	3 50	–	–	54.7
Potatoes, . . .	1 1-12	1,800	19 50	34.2	3.6	331.2
Beans, ...	4¾	95	4 50	22.0	2.0	51.0
Pease, ...	1⅔	30	50	6.9	0.5	15.7
Turnips, ...	5–6	90	75	0.8	0.2	4.6
Beets, ...	⅔	60	38	1.1	0.1	6.0
Cabbage, ...	1⅓	36	48	0.6	0.1	1.6
Apples, ...	1⅓	600	8 00	1.8	–	65.4
Raisins, ...	13	10	1 30	0.3	–	6.3
Total vegetable food, . .		4,643	$116 00	226.2	26.4	2,011.0
Total animal food, . .		3,949	252 50	284.0	742.8	97.8
Total food, . . .		8,592	$368 50	510.2	769.2	2,108.8
Meats, fish, etc., per man per day, ...		.98	$0 10	.11	.30	–
Dairy products and eggs, per man per day, . . .		1.29	05	.05	.13	.06
Animal food, per man per day,		2.27	$0 15	.16	.43	.06
Vegetable food, " "		2.66	07	.13	.01	1.15
Total food, " " .		4.93	$0 22	.29	.44	1.21

DIETARY NUMBER, A 5.

Description: Boarding-house in Lowell, Mass., of 150 persons, 75 males and 75 females. Boarders, mill operatives. Price of board per week for males, $2.45; for females, $2.05. Time, one month. Estimated as equivalent in demands for nutrients to 135 men for 30 days, or 1 man for 4,050 days.

ANALYSIS.

Kinds.	Prices per lb.	Quantities.	Costs.	Protein.	Fats.	Carbohydrates.
	cents.	lbs.		lbs.	lbs.	lbs.
Beef, roast, ...	10	400	$40 00	71.6	49.2	–
Beef steak, ...	14	290	40 60	52.8	35.7	–
Beef, corned, ...	10	420	42 00	51.2	103.7	–
Veal, ...	11	200	22 00	30.4	11.2	–
Lamb, ...	10	150	15 00	20.4	35.7	–
Pork, roast, ...	9	300	27 00	34.2	108.6	–
Salt pork, ...	10	100	10 00	2.8	76.5	–
Ham, ...	10	300	30 00	43.8	102.9	–
Lard, ...	7½	150	11 25	–	148.5	–
Haddock, ...	7	155	10 85	12.9	0.2	–
Cod, ...	7	75	5 25	8.3	0.2	–
Total meats, fish, etc., . . .		2,540	$253 95	328.4	672.4	–
Eggs (80 doz. at 21 cts.), . .	15¼	110	$16 80	12.8	11.2	0.7
Milk (2,000 qts. at 4 cts.), . .	2	4,000	80 00	136.0	148.0	192.0
Butter, ...	20	350	70 00	3.5	306.3	1.8
Cheese, ...	10	50	5 00	13.6	17.8	1.2
Total dairy products and eggs, ...		4,510	$171 80	165.9	483.3	195.7
Flour, ...	3¼	2,744	$89 18	304.6	30.4	2,060.0
Graham meal, ...	2½	100	2 50	11.7	1.7	69.9
Corn meal, ...	3	50	1 50	4.5	1.9	34.5
Oatmeal, ...	4	125	5 00	18.9	8.0	84.0
Beans (2½ bush. at $1.75), .	3	150	4 37	34.8	3.2	80.6
Rice, ...	8	20	1 60	1.5	0.1	15.8
Potatoes (48 bush. at 55 cts.), .	9-10	2,880	26 40	54.7	5.8	529.9
Cabbage (4 bbls. at $1.00), .	⅔	600	4 00	10.2	1.2	26.4
Onions (2 bush. at $1.00), .	2	104	2 00	1.0	0.2	7.8
Beets (2 bush. at 50 cts.), .	5-6	120	1 00	2.2	0.1	12 0
Turnips (2 bush. at 50 cts.), .	5-6	120	1 00	1.1	0.2	6.1
Squash, ...	2	100	2 00	0.5	0.1	5.3
Apples (10 bbls. at $1.25), .	¾	1,500	12 50	4.5	–	163.5
Sugar (230 lbs. at 5¼ cts.; 654 lbs. at 7½ cts.), . . .	5¼ and 7½	884	61 70	–	–	854.8
Molasses (8 gals. at 45 cts.), .	4 1-10	88	3 00	–	–	62.5
Corn starch, ...	8½	12	1 02	–	–	10.0
Crackers, ...	6	24	1 44	2.6	2.4	16.5
Soda crackers, ...	12½	20	2 50	2.0	1 9	14.1
Raisins, ...	11½	15	1 72	0.4	0.1	9.5
Total vegetable food, . .		9,656	$225 03	455.2	58.2	4,072.3
Total animal food, . .		7,050	425 75	494.3	1,155.7	195.7
Total food, ...		16,706	$650 78	949.5	1,213.9	4,268.0
Meats, fish, etc., per man per day, ...		.63	$0 06	.08	.17	–
Dairy products and eggs, per man per day, ...		1.11	04	.04	.12	.05
Animal food, per man per day,		1.74	$0 10	.12	.29	.05
Vegetable food, " " .		2.38	06	.11	.01	1.00
Total food, " " .		4.12	$0 16	.23	.30	1.05

The "Beef, roast" and "beef steak" in this dietary were both from the round, the latter from the uppermost, and the former from the next lower part, but both included in what is called in our analyses "first cut, round," the composition of which is, accordingly, assumed for both. The quantity of cabbages is stated at 4 barrels, costing $4.00. It is assumed that the weight would be 150 pounds per barrel, or 600 pounds in all, which would make the price ⅔ cents per pound.

DIETARY NUMBER, A 7.

Description: Boarding-house in Lynn, Mass., of 36 persons, 20 males and 16 females. Boarders, operatives in shoe factory, clerks, and dressmakers. Time, one month. Estimated as equivalent in demands for nutrients to 33 men for 30 days, or 1 man for 990 days.

ANALYSIS.

	FOOD-MATERIALS.				NUTRIENTS.		
Kinds.	Prices per lb.	Quanti- ties.	Costs.		Protein.	Fats.	Carbohy- drates.
	cents.	lbs.			lbs.	lbs.	lbs.
Beef, hip sirloin, . . .	28	114.8	$32 13		14.4	19.1	—
Beef, socket and rump, .	20	20	4 00		2.3	5.3	—
Beef, second cut, chuck ribs, .	10½	79	8 29		12.9	12.8	—
Beef, second cut, chuck ribs, .	11	42.3	4 65		6.9	6.9	—
Beef, ribs, ...	16	14	2 24		1.7	4.0	—
Beef, brisket, shoulder clod, and cross ribs, . . .	8	143.5	11 48		10.9	37.2	—
Mutton, ...	21½	21	4 52		3.2	3.3	—
Veal, ...	16	14.7	2 36		2.2	0.8	—
Salt pork, ...	11	25	2 75		0.7	19.1	—
Ham, ...	12	60	7 20		8.9	20.6	—
Lard, ...	10	57	5 70		—	56.4	—
Haddock, ...	6	25	1 50		2.1	—	—
Halibut, ...	12	50	6 00		7.6	2.1	—
Salt fish (cod), . . .	4½	40	1 80		6.4	0.2	—
Total meats, fish, etc., . .	. .	706.3	$94 62		89.1	187.8	—
Eggs (64 doz. at 20 cts.), .	14½	88	$12 80		10.2	9.0	0.5
Milk (352 qts. at 6 cts.), .	3	704	21 12		23.9	26.1	35.8
Cheese, ...	12	20	2 40		5.4	7.1	0.5
Butter, ...	23	89	20 47		0.9	77.9	0.5
Total dairy products and eggs, ...	. .	901	$56 79		40.4	120.1	35.3
Flour, ...	3	490	$14 70		54.4	5.4	369.5
Rye meal, ...	4	25	1 00		1.7	0.2	19.6
Oatmeal, ...	3	30	90		4.5	2.1	20.2
Rice, ...	10	2	20		0.1	—	1.6
Beans (13 qts.), . . .	3⅔	33.7	1 26		7.8	0.7	18.1
Potatoes (21 bush. at 67 cts.), .	1½	1,260	14 07		23.9	2.5	231.8
Turnips (1 bush.), . .	1⅔	60	1 00		0.5	0.1	3.1
Cabbage (6 heads at 8 cts.), .	⅔	36	48		0.6	0.1	1.6
Onions (1 pk.), . . .	2	13	25		0.1	—	1.0
Beets (2 bush.), . . .	⅔	120	80		2.2	0.1	12.0
Green pease (8 bush.), .	6	200	12 00		6.8	0.8	24.4
Pole beans (6 bush.), . .	4	150	6 00		4.2	0.5	15.0
Green corn (24 doz. ears at 12 cts.), ...	2⅔	108	2 88		5.0	2.1	37.4
Apples (4 bbls.), . . .	2	600	12 00		1.8	—	65.4
Corn starch, ...	8	12	96		—	—	10.0
Sugar, ...	6½	204	13 26		—	—	197.3
Molasses (2 gals.), . .	3⅔	22	80		—	—	15.6
Raisins, ...	10	15	1 50		0.4	0.1	9.5

DIETARY NUMBER, A 7—Concluded.

FOOD-MATERIALS.				NUTRIENTS.		
Kinds.	Prices per lb.	Quanti-ties.	Costs.	Protein.	Fats.	Carbohy-drates.
	cents.	lbs.		lbs.	lbs.	lbs.
Crackers, oyster, . . .	6	24	$1 20	3.0	1.2	18.4
Crackers, Boston, . . .	10	36	3 60	3.9	3.6	24.7
Total vegetable food, . . .		3,440.7	$88 86	120.9	19.5	1,096.2
Total animal food, . . .		1,607.3	151 41	129.5	307.9	35.3
Total food, ...		5,048.0	$240 27	250.4	327.4	1,131.5
Meats, fish, etc., per man per day, ...		.71	$0 10	.09	.19	–
Dairy products and eggs, per man per day, ...		.01	05	.04	.12	.04
Animal food, per man per day,		1.62	$0 15	.13	.31	.04
Vegetable food, " " .		3.48	09	.12	.02	1.11
Total food, " " .		5.10	$0 24	.25	.33	1.15

This dietary includes 24 dozen ears of green corn at 12 cents per dozen; 6 heads of cabbage at 8 cents per head; 8 bushels of green pease at $1.50 per bushel, and 6 bushels of pole beans at $1.00 per bushel.

The amounts of nutrients contained in these articles are estimated as follows: The ears of green corn are reported as weighing from ¼ pound to ½ pound each. Taking ⅜ pound as the average the 288 ears would weigh 108 pounds. A few analyses of " immature sweet corn " have been reported,* but, unfortunately, neither the proportion of kernel to cob nor the percentages of water in the kernel in the fresh state are given.

The composition of the air-dry kernel of a specimen harvested August 25th, in the condition in which it is commonly eaten for " green corn," was, however, nearly the same as that of the same corn harvested when mature, September 25th. The kernels of matured corn, in general, average about four-fifths of the weight of the whole ear, though the kernel of a specimen of sweet corn has been observed to make only about three-fourths of the weight of the ear.† A specimen of mature Ohio Dent corn was observed to shrink from about 125 pounds, when harvested, to 100 pounds when air-dry, and to contain

---

* By Johnson and Jenkins. Report of Connecticut Agricultural Experiment Station, 1878, pp. 59 and 68.

† *Ibid.*, page 74.

in the latter condition 10.8 per cent of water. Supposing the air-dry ears to have contained one-fifth by weight of cob, the 100 pounds of air-dry corn would have been contained in 125 pounds of air-dry ears. If kernel and cob both had lost in the same proportion in drying, that is, about one-fifth, making the air-dry ears four-fifths the weight of the fresh ears, the 125 pounds of air-dry ears, thus computed to furnish 100 pounds of corn, would have weighed when harvested 156 pounds. In other words, 156 pounds of the ears as harvested would have furnished 100 pounds of air-dry kernels, or 100 pounds of ears as harvested would supply 64 pounds of air-dry corn. Very likely as good a guess would be that 100 pounds of ears of green corn would furnish 50 pounds of air-dry kernels as any that could be afforded by these data. Though the sweet corn, so commonly used for green corn, is, as already stated, somewhat different in composition from ordinary corn and from the meal ground from it, we shall in the lack of more definite data estimate the ears of green corn as furnishing nutrients equivalent to those of half their weight of average corn meal. This is done here and elsewhere where sweet corn occurs. That is to say, the 288 ears of sweet corn of this dietary are computed to weigh $\frac{3}{8}$ of a pound each, or 108 pounds, and to be equivalent to 54 pounds of corn meal of the composition stated in the table of assumed composition of foods.

With less data for the estimate, we have taken the bushel of green pease and the bushel of pole beans as each furnishing 25 pounds of seeds and have assumed for both the composition of " sugar pea," reported by S. Moulton Babcock.*

---

* Report of New York Agricultural Experiment Station, 1884, page 333.

Dietary Number, A 9.

Description: Family in Boston, Mass., of 2 persons, husband and wife. Husband, a machinist, with $10.50 per week wages. Time, one month. Estimated as equivalent in demands for nutrients to 1.8 men at moderate work for 30 days, or 1 man for 54 days.

ANALYSIS.

Food-Materials.				Nutrients.		
Kinds.	Prices per lb.	Quantities.	Costs.	Protein.	Fats.	Carbohydrates.
	cents.	lbs.		lbs.	lbs.	lbs.
Beef steak,	28	28	$7 84	4.1	4.4	-
Beef, corned,	12	10	1 20	1.2	2.9	-
Lamb chop,	15	6	90	0.9	1.4	-
Salt pork,	12	2.5	30	0.1	1.9	-
Lard,	11	5	55	-	5.0	-
Halibut,	13	10	1 30	1.5	0.4	-
Mackerel,	5	12	60	1.2	0.5	-
Total meats, fish, etc.,	. .	73.5	$12 69	9.0	16.5	-
Eggs,	16	8.3	$1 32	1.0	0.8	0.1
Milk,	3½	70	2 45	2.4	2.6	3.4
Cheese,	13	2.5	32	0.7	0.9	0.1
Butter,	30	8	2 40	0.1	7.0	-
Total dairy products and eggs,	. .	88.8	$6 49	4.2	11.3	3.6
Flour,	4	30	$1 20	3.3	0.3	22.6
Beans,	6	3.7	20	0.9	0.1	2.0
Rice,	8	1	08	0.1	-	0.8
Potatoes,	1¼	30	38	0 6	0.1	5.5
Apples,	1⅔	15	25	-	-	1.6
Vegetables,	-	112.6	2 00	2.1	0.3	9.7
Sugar,	7½	18	1 35	-	-	17.4
Molasses,	6	1.5	09	-	-	1.1
Corn starch,	10	0.5	05	-	-	0 4
Raisins,	12	1	12	-	-	0.6
Crackers,	4	12	48	1.3	1.2	8.2
Total vegetable food,	. .	225.3	$6 20	8.3	2.0	69.9
Total animal food,	. .	162.3	10 18	13.2	27.8	3.6
Total food,	. .	387.6	$25 38	21.5	29.8	73.5
Meats, fish, etc., per man per day,	. .	1.36	$0 24	.17	.31	-
Dairy products and eggs, per man per day,	. .	1.64	12	.08	.21	.07
Animal food, per man per day,	. .	3.00	$0 36	.25	.52	.07
Vegetable food, " "	. .	4.17	11	.15	.04	1.29
Total food, " "	. .	7.17	$0 47	.40	.56	1.36

In numbers A 9 and A 11, the kinds and quantities of vegetables are not given, the cost only being stated. The quantities are, however, small, so that even a considerable error might be made in estimating the quantities of nutrients without materially affecting the final result. An estimate has been made by the same method as was followed in A 14, A 15, and A 16, taking as data the kinds, amounts, and costs of vegetables in the other dietaries of this series (exclusive of those of French Canadians), and assuming that the averages of the latter would represent the kinds, quantities, and costs of the vegetables in these two dietaries. The calculation is rather complex and the details are not inserted here.

DIETARY NUMBER, A 11.

Description: Family in East Cambridge, Mass., of 6 persons, 3 adults and 3 children, the latter of 5, 11, and 12 years respectively. Two of the adults are females; the third, the father of the family, is a glass-blower, with exhausting work, and receiving $24 per week wages. Time, one week. Estimated as equivalent in demands for nutrients to 4½ men for 7 days, or 1 man for 32 days.

ANALYSIS.

Kinds.	FOOD-MATERIALS.			NUTRIENTS.		
	Prices per lb.	Quantities.	Costs.	Protein.	Fats.	Carbohydrates.
	cents.	lbs.		lbs.	lbs.	lbs.
Beef steak, ...	28	6	$1 68	0.8	1.0	–
Lamb, ...	15	5	75	0.7	1.2	–
Salt pork, ...	10	1	10	–	0.8	–
Lard, ...	10	1	10	–	1.0	–
Mackerel, ...	4	8	32	0.8	0.3	–
Total meats, fish, etc., . .		21	$2 95	2.3	4.3	–
Eggs (1 doz. at 23 cts.), .	16	1.4	$0 23	0.2	0.1	0.1
Milk (10 qts. at 7 cts.), . .	3½	20	70	0.7	0.7	1.0
Cheese, ...	12	0.7	08	0.2	0.3	–
Butter, ...	30	4	1 20	–	3.5	–
Total dairy products and eggs, ...		26.1	$2 21	1.1	4.6	1.1
Flour, ...	3½	14	$0 49	1.6	0.2	10.6
Beans (1¼ qts.), . .	6	2.5	15	0.6	0.1	1.3
Pease, ...	15	1	15	0.2	–	0.5
Rice, ...	8	1	08	0.1	–	0.8
Potatoes (½ bush.), .	1¼	30	38	0.6	0.1	5.5
Apples (1 pk.), . .	2	15	30	–	–	1.6
Vegetables, . . .	–	18.7	35	0.2	–	1.6
Sugar, ...	7½	8	60	–	–	7.7
Molasses (1 qt.), . .	5	3	15	–	–	2.1
Raisins, ...	12	1	12	–	–	0.6
Crackers, ...	6	1	06	0.1	0.1	0.7
Total vegetable food, . .		95.2	$2 83	3.4	0.5	33.0
Total animal food, . .		47.1	5 16	3.4	8.9	1.1
Total food, . . .		142.3	$7 99	6.8	9.4	34.1
Meats, fish, etc., per man per day, ...		.66	$0 09	.07	.13	–
Dairy products and eggs, per man per day, . .		.82	07	.03	.14	.03
Animal food, per man per day,		1.48	$0 16	.10	.27	.03
Vegetable food, " "		2.97	09	.11	.02	1.03
Total food, " " .		4.45	$0 25	.21	.29	1.06

DIETARY NUMBER, A 13.

Description : Boarding-house in Lawrence, Mass., of 80 persons, 40 males and 40 females. Boarders, mill operatives. Price of board per week for males, $3.00; for females, $2.00. Estimated to require nutrients equal to 72 men at moderate work for 30 days, or 1 man for 2,160 days.

ANALYSIS.

Kinds.	Prices per lb.	Quanti-ties.	Costs.	Protein.	Fats.	Carbohy-drates.
	cents.	lbs.		lbs.	lbs.	lbs.
Beef, roast,	8	275	$22 00	44.8	44.6	–
Beef, corned,	8	291	23 28	32.9	83.8	–
Beef steak,	14	263	36.82	47.0	32.3	–
Beef tongue,	16	14.3	2 28	2.1	2.2	–
Veal,	11	111.5	12 26	16.9	6.2	–
Lamb, roast,	10	56	5 60	7.6	13.3	–
Ham,	10	186	18 60	27.1	63.8	–
Sausage,	10	10	1 00	1.3	3.0	–
Pork, roast,	8½	254	21 59	28.9	91.0	–
Salt pork,	10	50	5 00	1.4	38.3	–
Lard,	9	135	12 15	–	133.7	–
Haddock,	6	160	9 60	13.3	0.2	–
Halibut,	12	75	9 00	11.3	3.2	–
Salt fish (cod),	4½	30	1 35	4.8	0.1	–
Total meats, fish, etc.,		1,910.8	$180 53	239.4	517.5	–
Eggs (160 doz. at 16 cts.),	11⅚	220	$25 60	25.5	22.4	1.3
Milk (1,570 qts. at 4 cts.),	2	3,140	62 80	100.6	116.2	150.7
Butter,	13	262.5	34 12	2.6	229.7	1.3
Cheese,	10	44	4 40	11.0	15.6	1.0
Total dairy products and eggs,		3,666.5	$126 92	146.6	383.0	154.3
Flour,	3	784	$23 52	87.0	8.7	591.1
Oatmeal,	3	80	2 40	12.1	5.7	53.8
Tapioca,	7	10	70	0.1	–	8.5
Beans (72 qts. at 6 cts.),	3 1-5	135	4 32	31.3	2.8	72.5
Rice,	7	5	35	0.4	–	4.0
Potatoes (60 bush. at 55 cts.),	11-12	3,600	33 00	68.4	7.2	602.4
Squash,	3	61.5	1 85	3.1	0.1	3.3
Lettuce (27 heads at 2½ cts.),	5	13.5	67	0.2	–	0.3
Onions (½ bush.),	4	26	1 00	0.3	0.1	2.0
Tomatoes (1 bush.),	2⅓	60	1 40	0.8	0.2	2.7
Green corn (20 doz. cars at 14 cts.),	3 1-9	90	2 80	4.1	1.7	31.1
Apples (2 bbls. at $2.50),	1⅚	300	5 00	0.9	–	32.7
Sugar,	7½	804	60 30	–	–	777.5
Molasses (8 gals. at 28 cts.),	2½	88	2 24	–	–	62.5
Raisins,	9	30	2 70	0.8	0.2	18.0
Total vegetable food,		6,087	$142 25	209.5	26.7	2,323.3
Total animal food,		5,577.3	307 45	386.0	901.4	154.3
Total food,		11,664.3	$449 70	595.5	928.1	2,477.6
Meats, fish, etc., per man per day,		.88	$0 08	.11	.24	–
Dairy products and eggs, per man per day,		1.70	06	.07	.18	.07
Animal food, per man per day,		2.58	$0 14	.18	.42	.07
Vegetable food, " "		2.81	07	.10	.01	1.08
Total food, " "		5.39	$0 21	.28	.43	1.15

This dietary includes 20 dozen ears of corn at 14 cents per dozen, and 27 heads of lettuce at $2\frac{1}{2}$ cents per head. On the basis of information obtained from dealers the corn is estimated to weigh from $\frac{1}{4}$ pound to $\frac{1}{2}$ pound per ear and the lettuce $\frac{1}{2}$ pound per head. Taking $\frac{3}{8}$ pound for the average weight of the ears of corn the 240 ears would weigh 90 pounds and the corn on them would be equivalent to 45 pounds of corn meal.

DIETARY NUMBER, A 14.

Description: French Canadian family in North Cambridge, Mass., consisting of 4 persons, father, mother, and two children of 2 and 3 years respectively. The father is employed in a brick yard, at severe labor. Wages, $30 per month. Time, one month. The two children are taken as equivalent to one woman, making the family equivalent in demands for nutrients to 2.6 men at moderate work for 30 days, or 1 man for 78 days.

ANALYSIS.

Kinds.	Prices per lb.	Quantities.	Costs.	Protein.	Fats.	Carbohydrates.
	cents.	lbs.		lbs.	lbs.	lbs.
Pork, steak,	10	22	$2 20	2.5	8.0	–
Pork, corned, shoulder,	10	25	2 50	2.7	0.0	–
Pork, salt,	10	8	80	0.2	6.1	–
Lard,	10	5	50	–	5.0	–
Salt fish (cod),	4½	10	45	1.6	–	–
Total meats, fish, etc.,		70	$6 45	7.0	29.0	–
Milk,	3½	40	$1 40	1.4	1.5	1.9
Eggs,	16	6.3	90	0.7	0.6	–
Butter,	28	9	2 52	0.1	7.9	–
Total dairy products and eggs,		55.3	$4 91	2.2	10.0	1.9
Flour,	3½	55	$1 92	6.1	0.6	41.5
Beans,	5½	7.5	40	1.7	0.2	4.0
Rice,	8	5	40	0.4	–	4.0
Potatoes,	1 1-12	120	1 30	2.3	0.2	22.1
Vegetables,	–	199.4	2 50	2.8	0.4	10.3
Sugar,	8	26	2 08	–	–	25.1
Molasses,	4½	27.5	1 25	–	–	19.5
Total vegetable food,		440.4	$9 85	13.3	1.4	126.5
Total animal food,		125.3	11 36	9.2	39.0	1.9
Total food,		565.7	$21 21	22.5	40.4	128.4
Meats, fish, etc., per man per day,		.90	$0 08	.09	.37	–
Dairy products and eggs, per man per day,		.71	06	.03	.13	.03
Animal food, per man per day,		1.61	$0 14	.12	.50	.03
Vegetable food, " "		5.65	13	.17	.02	1.62
Total food, " "		7.26	$0 27	.29	·.52	1.65

DIETARY NUMBER, A 15.

Description: French Canadian family in North Cambridge, Mass., consisting of father, mother, and three children of 5, 4, and 2 years respectively. The father is employed in a brick yard, at severe labor. Wages, $30 per month. Time, one month. Estimated as equivalent in demands for nutrients to 3⅓ men at moderate work for 30 days, or 1 man for 100 days.

ANALYSIS.

Kinds.	Prices per lb.	Quantities.	Costs.	Protein.	Fats.	Carbohydrates.
	cents.	lbs.		lbs.	lbs.	lbs.
Pork, steak, ...	10	20	$2 00	2.3	7.2	–
Pork, corned, shoulder, .	9	30	2 70	3.2	11.9	–
Pork, salt, ...	10	6	60	0.2	4.6	–
Lard, ...	10	4	40	–	4.0	–
Salt fish (cod), . . .	5	12	60	1.9	–	–
Total meats, fish, etc., .	. .	72	$6 30	7.6	27.7	–
Eggs (6 doz. at 20 cts.), .	14⅓	8.25	$1 20	1.0	0.9	0.1
Milk (15⅓ qts. at 7 cts.), .	3⅓	31	1 08	1.1	1.1	1.5
Butter, ...	30	8	2 40	0.1	7.0	–
Total dairy products and eggs, ...	. .	47.25	$4 68	2.2	9.0	1.6
Flour, ...	3⅓	66	$2 31	7.3	0.7	49.8
Rice, ...	8	4	32	0.3	–	3.2
Beans (2 qts. at 10 cts.), .	5⅓	3.8	20	0.9	0.1	2.0
Potatoes (1⅓ bush. at 75 cts.), .	1⅓	90	1 13	1.7	0.2	17.0
Vegetables, ...	–	159.4	2 00	2.2	0.2	8.2
Sugar, ...	8	24	1 92	–	–	23.2
Molasses (2 gals. at 50 cts.), .	4⅓	22	1 00	–	–	15.6
Total vegetable food, . .	. .	369.2	$8 88	12.4	1.2	119.0
Total animal food, . .	. .	119.25	10 98	9.8	36.7	1.6
Total food, . . .	. .	488.45	$19 86	22.2	37.9	120.6
Meats, fish, etc., per man per day, ...	. .	.72	$0 06	.08	.28	–
Dairy products and eggs, per man per day, . . .	. .	.47	05	.02	.09	.01
Animal food, per man per day,	. .	1.19	$0 11	.10	.37	.01
Vegetable food, " "	. .	3.69	09	.12	.01	1.19
Total food, " "	. .	4.88	$0 20	.22	.38	1.20

DIETARY NUMBER, A 16.

Description: French Canadian family in North Cambridge, Mass., consisting of husband, wife, and three children of 1, 2, and 4 years, respectively. The husband is employed at severe labor in a brick yard. Wages, $30 per month. Time, one month. Estimated as equivalent in demands for nutrients to 3 men at moderate work for 30 days, or 1 man for 90 days.

ANALYSIS.

Kinds.	Prices per lb.	Quantities.	Costs.	Protein.	Fats.	Carbohydrates.
	cents.	lbs.		lbs.	lbs.	lbs.
Beef, corned, ...	10	15	$1 50	1.7	4.3	–
Pork steak, ...	13	12	1 56	1.4	4.3	–
Pork, salt, ...	11	5.5	61	0.2	4.2	–
Lard, ...	11	6	66	–	6.0	–
Mackerel, ...	10	6	60	0.6	0.2	–
Total meats, fish, etc., .	. .	44.5	$4 93	3.9	19.0	–

DIETARY NUMBER, A 16 — Concluded.

	FOOD-MATERIALS.				NUTRIENTS.		
Kinds.	Prices per lb.	Quanti-ties.	Costs.		Protein.	Fats.	Carbohy-drates.
	cents.	lbs.			lbs.	lbs.	lbs.
Eggs (4½ doz. at 19 cts.), .	14	6.2	$0 86		0.7	0.6	–
Milk (20 qts at 7 cts.), . .	3½	40	1 40		1.4	1.5	1.9
Butter, ...	25	5	1 25		0.1	4.4	–
Cheese, ...	12	4	48		1.1	1.4	0.1
Total dairy products and eggs, ...	. .	55.2	$3 99		3.3	7.9	2.0
Flour, ...	3¼	65	$2 11		7.2	0.7	49.0
Potatoes (1 bush. at 70 cts.), .	1 1-6	60	70		1.1	0.1	11.0
Beans (3 qts. at 9 cts.), . .	5	5.6	27		1.3	0.1	3.0
Rice, ...	8	2	16		0.1	–	1.6
Vegetables, . . .	–	79.7	1 00		1.2	0.1	4.1
Sugar, ...	6	15.5	93		–	–	15.0
Molasses, (1 gal.), . .	5½	11	60		–	–	7.8
Raisins, ...	12	2	24		0.1	–	1.3
Crackers, . . .	5	10	50		1.1	1.0	6.9
Total vegetable food, . .	. .	250.8	$6 51		12.1	2.0	99.7
Total animal food, . .	. .	99.7	8 92		7.2	26.9	2.0
Total food, . . .	. .	350.5	$15 43		19.3	28.9	101.7
Meats, fish, etc., per man per day, ...	.	.49	$0 06		.04	.21	–
Dairy products and eggs, per man per day, ...	.	.61	04		.04	.09	.02
Animal food, per man per day, .	.	1.10	$0 10		.08	.30	.02
Vegetable food, " " .	.	2.79	07		.13	.02	1.11
Total food, " " .	.	3.89	$0 17		.21	.32	1.13

In numbers A 14, A 15, and A 16 the costs of the vegetables are given without statement of the kinds and quantities.
As these are all of French Canadian families it may not be far
out of the way to assume that the vegetables would be similar
to those of series B which are, likewise, dietaries of French
Canadians in Massachusetts. By a computation, of which the
details would be too lengthy for this place, the kinds, quantities, and costs of the vegetables of the dietaries of series B
have been taken and an estimate has been made of the average
quantities of vegetables (cabbages, onions, turnips, squash,
etc.,) obtained for one dollar and the amounts, of nutrients in
each, and in the whole dollar's worth. The estimated total
quantities (of vegetables) and quantities of nutrients are stated
in A 16 in which the vegetables cost $1.00. In A 14 in which
the cost of the vegetables was $2.50, or 2½ times the cost in A
16, and in A 15 in which the vegetables cost $2.00, or twice
the cost in A 16, these quantities are assumed.

Series B.   French Canadian, Massachusetts.

The five dietaries of this series which are used in the analyses
tables include those of three families and two boarding-houses
in Holyoke, Lawrence, and Lowell.   Of those included only
in the averages, two were of families in Worcester, of this
series, and three of families in East Cambridge, of series A.
With the exception of women, children, and others engaged
in household duties, or in no actual labor, the people are
mostly mill and factory operatives; a few are brickmakers.

DIETARY NUMBER, B 1.

Description: French Canadian family in Lawrence, Mass., consisting of father, mother, and
four children, a daughter of 17½ and three sons, 16, 19, and 21 years of age, respectively, making,
in all, 6 adults, 4 males and 2 females, of which the four children are mill operatives, the father
and mother doing no considerable amount of outside work.   The sons earn from $1.25 to $1.75
per day, and the daughter 90 cents.   Time, one month.   Estimated as equivalent in demands
for food to 5½ laboring men for 30 days, or 1 man for 165 days.

ANALYSIS.

Kinds.	FOOD-MATERIALS.				NUTRIENTS.		
	Prices per lb.	Quanti-ties.	Costs.		Protein.	Fats.	Carbohy-drates.
	cents.	lbs.			lbs.	lbs.	lbs.
Beef, ...	–	68	} $20 00		9.1	16.5	–
Pork, fresh, ...	–	42			4.8	15.2	–
Salt pork, ...	–	14			0.4	10.7	–
Lard, ...	9	10	90		–	9.9	–
Fish (salt mackerel), . .	10	17.5	1 75		2.6	2.6	–
Total meats, fish, etc., .	. .	151.5	$22 65		16.9	54.9	–
Eggs (10 doz. at 20 cts.), .	14½	13.8	$2 00		1.6	1.4	0.1
Milk, ...	3 2-5	88	3 00		3.0	3.3	4.2
Butter, ...	28	8	2 25		0.1	7.0	–
Total dairy products and eggs, ...	. .	109.8	$7 25		4.7	11.7	4.3
Flour, ...	4 1.56	112	$4 50		12.4	1.2	84.4
Beans (5 qts. at 10 cts.), .	5½	9.4	50		2.2	0.2	5.0
Pease (3 qts. at 8½ cts.), .	4½	5 6	25		1.3	0.1	2.9
Barley, ...	6½	5.5	36		0.5	–	4.3
Rice, ...	8	5.5	44		0.4	–	4.4
Potatoes, ...	1½	120	1 75		2.3	0.2	22 0
Apples, ...	1¾	75	1 25		0.2	–	8.2
Vegetables, ...	–	110	1 50		1.0	0.1	6.7
Corn starch, ...	10	3	30		–	–	2 5
Molasses and syrup, . .	7-10	17.3	1 25		–	–	12.3
Sugar, ...	7⅖	30	2 30		–	–	29.0
Raisins and currants, . .	12½	4	50		0.1	–	2.5
Total vegetable food, . .	. .	497.3	$14 90		20.4	1.8	184.2
Total animal food, . .	. .	261.3	29 90		21.6	66.6	4.3
Total food, . . .	. .	758.6	$44 80		42.0	68.4	188.5
Meats, fish, etc., per man per day, ...	. .	.92	$0 14		.10	.33	–
Dairy products and eggs, per man per day, . . .	. .	.66	04		.03	.07	.03
Animal food, per man per day,	. .	1.58	$0 18		.13	.40	.03
Vegetable food, " "	. .	3.01	09		.12	.01	1.12
Total food, " "	. .	4.59	$0 27		.25	.41	1.15

The meat is given as 124 lbs., costing $20.00, and is stated in an explanatory note to be about 50 or 60 per cent of beef and the remainder pork, of which one-fourth is fresh and three-fourths salt. The fish is inferred to be salt mackerel. The vegetables stated to cost $1.50 are said to consist of cabbages, about 40 per cent; onions, 20 per cent; turnips, 10 per cent; carrots, 5 per cent; the remainder, 25 per cent, varying with the season.

The following quantities of vegetables at the prices assumed would cost $1.50:

Vegetables.	Per cent.	Quantity.	Price per lb.	Cost.
		lbs.	cts.	
Cabbages, ...	40	44	1¼	$0 55
Onions, ...	20	22	2	44
Turnips, ...	10	11	1	11
Carrots, ...	5	5	1	05
Remainder, ...	25	28	1¼	35
Totals, ...	100	110	–	$1 50

The nutrients in the vegetables are estimated by comparison of the amounts thus computed with the composition as given in the table of composition of vegetable foods.

The mixture of barley and rice is said to contain about equal parts of both, the former costing about six, and the latter eight, cents per pound.

Dietary Number, B 4.

Description: Boarding-house, Holyoke, Mass. French Canadian. Eighteen persons, 3 children and 15 adults (8 men and 7 women). Operatives in paper mills. The wages of the men are about $1.25 per day, and of the women, 90 cents. The price of board per week is $2.75 for men and $2.00 for women. Time, one month. Estimated as equivalent in demands for nutrients to 15½ men for 30 days, or 1 man for 465 days.

ANALYSIS.

Food-Materials.				Nutrients.		
Kinds.	Prices per lb.	Quanti- ties.	Costs.	Protein.	Fats.	Carbohy- drates.
	cents.	lbs.		lbs.	lbs.	lbs.
Beef, ...	–	200 ⎫		25.8	84.2	–
Veal, ...	–	20 ⎟	$45 00	3 0	1.1	–
Mutton, ...	–	20 ⎬		2.8	4.7	–
Pork, fresh, ...	–	60 ⎭		6.8	21.7	–
Salt pork, ...	9	100	9 00	2.8	76.5	–
Lard, ...	10	40	4 00	–	39.6	–
Total meats, etc., . .	.	.	$58 00	41.2	227.8	–

DIETARY NUMBER, B 4 — Concluded.

FOOD-MATERIALS.				NUTRIENTS.		
Kinds.	Prices per lb.	Quanti- ties.	Costs.	Protein.	Fats.	Carbohy- drates.
	cents.	lbs.		lbs.	lbs.	lbs.
Eggs (50 doz. at 18 cts.), . .	13 1-12	68.8	$9 00	8.0	7.0	0.4
Milk (136 qts.), ...	3½	272	9 00	9.2	10.1	13.1
Butter, ...	27	30	8 10	0.3	26.3	0.2
Total dairy products and eggs, ...	. .	370.8	$26 10	17.5	43.4	13.7
Flour, ...	5	120	$6 00	13.3	1.3	90.5
Beans (8 qts. at 7½ cts.), .	4	15	60	3.5	0.3	8.1
Pease (5 qts. at 8 cts.), . .	4½	9.4	40	2.2	0.1	4.9
Rice, ...	—	16.1 ⎰	1 40	1.2	0.1	12.8
Barley, ...	—	6.9 ⎱		0.6	0.1	5.4
Potatoes, ...	1½	420	6 00	8.0	0.8	77.3
Vegetables, ...	—	594	8 01	8.3	1.2	31.4
Corn starch, ...	10	4	40	—	—	3.3
Sugar, ...	7½	60	4 50	—	—	58.0
Syrup and molasses, . .	½	40.2	2 00	—	—	28.5
Total vegetable food, . .	. .	1,285.6	$29 31	37.1	3.9	320.2
Total animal food, . .	. .	810.8	84 10	58.7	271.2	13.7
Total food, . . .	. .	2,096.4	$113 41	95.8	275.1	333.9
Meats, etc., per man per day, .	. .	.95	$0 12	.09	.49	—
Dairy products and eggs, per man per day, ...	. .	.80	06	.04	.09	.03
Animal food, per man per day,	. .	1.75	$0 18	.13	.58	.03
Vegetable food, " " .	. .	2.76	06	.08	.01	.69
Total food, " " .	. .	4.51	$0 24	.21	.59	.72

The meat is said to consist of 300 pounds of fresh meat, costing $45.00, and 100 pounds of salt pork, costing $9.00. In an explanatory note the meat is estimated to consist usually of beef, 50 per cent; veal, 5 per cent; mutton, 5 per cent; and pork, 40 per cent, of which about two-thirds is fresh. This would make the total amount of salt pork equal 13⅓ per cent, whereas in the figures of the dietary it is said to make 100 pounds of the whole 400 pounds of meat, or just 25 per cent. Assuming, however, that the word fresh in the note was a slip of the pen, for salt, there would be 26⅔ per cent of salt pork, which coincides with the figures of the dietary. In the calculations it is assumed that only one-third of the pork is fresh.

The quantity of vegetables is not stated in the dietary. The cost is given at $8.00. The cabbages are estimated to make 60 per cent; onions, 20 per cent; turnips, 15 per cent; and car- rots, 5 per cent of the amount. Assuming the cost of the cab-hage to be 1¼ cents, of the onions 2 cents, and of the turnips and carrots 1 cent each per pound, $8.00 would buy the following quantities of vegetables :

VEGETABLES.	Per cent.	Quantity.	Price per lb.	Cost.
		lbs.	cts.	
Cabbages, ...	60	356	1¼	$4 45
Onions, ...	20	119	2	2 37
Turnips, ...	15	89	1	89
Carrots, ...	5	30	1	30
Totals, ...	100	594	–	$8 01

The quantities of nutrients ascribed to vegetables in the dietary are those estimated to occur in the above named quantities of cabbages, onions, turnips, and carrots.

The mixture of rice and barley is stated to contain about 70 per cent of rice and 30 per cent of barley.

DIETARY NUMBER, B 5.

Description : Boarding-house, Holyoke, Mass. French Canadians. Ten persons, 6 males and 4 females, from 16 to 40 years of age. Factory operatives. Time, one month. Wages, males, $1.25 to $1.50 per day; females, 90 cents to $1.00. Estimated as equivalent to 9⅓ men for 30 days, or 1 man for 280 days.

ANALYSIS.

FOOD-MATERIALS.				NUTRIENTS.		
Kinds.	Prices per lb.	Quanti- ties.	Costs.	Protein.	Fats.	Carbohy- drates.
	cents.	lbs.		lbs.	lbs.	lbs.
Beef, ...	–	42		5.2	12.9	–
Veal, ...	–	5	$27 40	0.8	0.3	–
Mutton, ...	–	5		0.7	1.2	–
Pork, fresh, . . .	–	119		13.5	43.0	–
Pork, salt, . . .	10	37.5	3 75	1.1	28.7	–
Lard, ...	10	40	4 00	–	40.0	–
Fish (salt mackerel), . .	10	46	4 50	6.6	6.8	–
Total meats, fish, etc., . .	. .	293.5	$39 65	27.9	132.9	–
Eggs (30 doz. at 13.2 cts.), .	13½	45	$6 00	5.2	4.6	0.3
Milk (20 qts. at 7½ cts.), .	3¾	40	1 50	1.4	1.5	1.9
Butter (26 lbs.), . . .	27	26	7 00	0.3	22.8	0.1
Total dairy products and eggs, ...	. .	111	$14 50	6.9	28.9	2.3
Flour, ...	4	300	$12 00	33.3	3.3	226.2
Barley, ...	–	0.4	30	–	–	0.3
Rice, ...	–	3.6		0.3	–	2.9
Beans (7 qts. at 8½ cts.), .	4¾	13	60	3.0	0.3	7.0
Pease (9 qts. at 8 cts.), .	4¼	17	72	3.9	0.3	8.9
Potatoes (6½ bush. at 88 cts.),	–	390	5 72	7.4	0.8	71.8
Vegetables, ...	–	465	6 00	7.3	.0.8	22.2
Total vegetable food, . .	. .	1,189	$25 34	55.2	5.5	339.3
Total animal food, . .	. .	404.5	54 15	34.8	161.8	2.3
Total food, . . .	. .	1,593.5	$79 49	90.0	167.3	341.6

DIETARY NUMBER, B 5 — Concluded.

FOOD-MATERIALS.				NUTRIENTS.		
Kinds.	Prices per lb.	Quanti-ties.	Costs.	Protein.	Fats.	Carbohy-drates.
Meats, fish, etc., per man per day, ...	cents. . .	lbs. 1.05	$0 14	lbs. .10	lbs. .47	lbs. –
Dairy products and eggs, per man per day, ...	. .	.39	05	.02	.10	.01
Animal food, per man per day,	. .	1.44	$0 19	.12	.57	.01
Vegetable food, " " .	. .	4.25	09	.19	.02	1.21
Total food, " " .	. .	5.69	$0 28	.31	.59	1.22

The meat was said to include 208½ pounds, costing $31.15, of which 37½ pounds were salt pork, costing $3.75, and 171 pounds fresh meat, costing $27.40. The whole meat was estimated to consist of beef, about 20 per cent; mutton and veal in equal parts, 5 per cent; and pork, fresh and salt, 75 per cent. The vegetables are reported to have been about 80 per cent of cabbage; 10 per cent, onions; and the rest turnips and carrots in nearly equal amounts. The amounts and composition of the vegetables are calculated as in the preceding dietaries, B 1 and B 4.

DIETARY NUMBER, B 6.

Description : French Canadian family in Holyoke, Mass., consisting of 6 persons, father, mother, and four children, aged 9, 12½, 17, and 24, of which the last two are counted as adults, making 4 adults and 2 children in the family. The two oldest children, one male and one female, are mill operatives, and earn respectively $1.35 and 90 cents per day. The father works occasionally, and earns $1.25 per day. Time, one month. Estimated as equivalent in demands for nutrients to 5 laboring men for 30 days, or 1 man for 150 days.

ANALYSIS.

FOOD-MATERIALS.				NUTRIENTS.		
Kinds.	Prices per lb.	Quanti-ties.	Costs.	Protein.	Fats.	Carbohy-drates.
	cents.	lbs.		lbs.	lbs.	lbs.
Beef, ...	–	25.2		3.4	6.3	–
Pork, fresh, ...	–	15.7		1.9	5.7	–
Mutton, ...	–	3.2	$9 45	0.4	0.8	–
Veal, ...	–	3.2		0.5	0.2	–
Salt pork, ...	–	15.7		0.5	12.0	–
Lard, ...	9	6.5	59	–	6.4	–
Total meats, etc., . . .	. .	69.5	$10 04	6.7	31.4	–
Eggs (13½ doz.), . . .	10¾	25.3	$2 70	2.9	2.6	0.2
Butter, ...	25	7	1 75	0.1	6.1	–
Total dairy products and eggs, ...	. .	32.3	$4 45	3.0	8.7	0.2

DIETARY NUMBER, B 6 — Concluded.

FOOD-MATERIALS.				NUTRIENTS.		
Kinds.	Prices per lb.	Quantities.	Costs.	Protein.	Fats.	Carbohydrates.
	cents.	lbs.		lbs.	lbs.	lbs.
Flour, ...	4	37	$1 50	4.1	0.4	27.9
Rice, ...	–	1.7 }	28	0.1	–	1.3
Barley, ...	–	1.8 }		0.2	–	1.4
Potatoes (1¼ bush.), . .	1¼	75	1 10	1.4	0.2	13.8
Vegetables, . . .	–	52.8	65	0.6	0.1	2.9
Corn starch, ...	11	2	22	–	–	1.7
Sugar, ...	8	21.5	1 72	–	–	20.8
Molasses and syrup, . .	–	34.5	1 58	–	–	24.5
Bread (63 two-pound loaves), .	2½	126	3 15	11.2	2.4	69.9
Total vegetable food, . .	. .	352.3	$10 20	17.6	3.1	164.2
Total animal food, . .	. .	101.8	14 49	9.7	40.1	0.2
Total food, . . .	. .	454.1	$24 69	27.3	43.2	164.4
Meats, etc., per man per day, .	. .	.46	$0 07	.04	.21	–
Dairy products and eggs, per man per day, ...	. .	.21	03	.02	.06	–
Animal food, per man per day,	. .	.67	$0 10	.06	.27	–
Vegetable food, " "	. .	2.35	07	.12	.02	1.09
Total food, " "	. .	3.02	$0 17	.18	.29	1.09

The meat is reported at 63 pounds, costing $9.45, and said to be about 40 per cent of beef; 5 per cent, mutton; 5 per cent, veal; 25 per cent, fresh pork; and 25 per cent, salt pork. The beef was said to be mostly brisket and shoulder.

The vegetables are reported to have cost 65 cents and to consist of about 50 per cent of cabbage; 20 per cent, turnips; 5 per cent, onions; 5 per cent, carrots; the remainder being "sundries, and varying according to the season." For the latter the composition of onions, which is about the average of all, is assumed.

The report includes 3½ pounds of rice, costing 28 cents, but a note appended implies that this is the mixture of rice and barley commonly used by Canadians and consisting, in this case, of one-half rice and one-half barley.

The amounts of vegetables are computed as below :

VEGETABLES.	Per cent.	Quantity.	Price per lb.	Cost.
		lbs.	cts.	
Cabbages, ...	50	26.4	1¼	$0 33
Turnips, ...	20	10.6	1	11
Onions, ...	5	2.6	2	5
Carrots, ...	5	2.6	1	3
Remainder, ...	20	10.6	1¼	13
Totals, ...	100	52.8	–	$0 65

DIETARY NUMBER, B 10.

Description: French Canadian family in Lowell, Mass., consisting of two brothers, black-smiths, and a sister, mill operative. One of the two blacksmiths states that he and his brother each cleared $600 last year. The sister states that she earns $1.00 per day when working in the mill. Time, one month. As the labor may be more severe than usual, the three persons are estimated as equivalent in demands for nutrients to 3 men for 30 days, or 1 man for 90 days.

ANALYSIS.

	FOOD-MATERIALS.				NUTRIENTS.		
Kinds.	Prices per lb.	Quanti-ties.	Costs.	Protein.	Fats.	Carbohy-drates.
	cents.	lbs.		lbs.	lbs.	lbs.
Beef,	–	57.7		8.1	17.0	–
Mutton,	–	11.5	$14 20	1.6	2.7	–
Pork, fresh,	–	28.8		3.3	10.4	–
Pork, salt,	10	17	1 70	0.5	13.0	–
Total meats,		115	$15 90	13.5	43.1	–
Eggs (23 doz. at 19 cts.),	14	31.6	$4 40	3.7	3.2	0.2
Milk (48 qts.),	3	96	3 06	3.3	3.6	4.6
Butter,	27	8	2 16	0.1	7.0	–
Total dairy products and eggs,		135.6	$9 62	7.1	13.8	4.8
Beans and pease (3½ qts.),	4	6.6	$0 27	1.5	0.1	3.5
Rice,	6⅞	4.5	40	0.3	–	3.6
Barley,		1.5		0.1	–	1.2
Potatoes (2 bush.),	1½	120	1 71	2.3	0.2	22.1
Vegetables,	–	66	90	0.9	0.1	2.7
Sugar,	6⅜	17	1 15	–	–	16.4
Molasses,	4½	22	98	–	–	15.6
Bread (79 two-pound loaves),	2½	158	3 95	14.1	3.0	87.7
Total vegetable food,		395.6	$9 36	19.2	3.4	152.9
Total animal food,		250.6	25 52	20.6	56.9	4.8
Total food,		646.2	$34 88	39.8	60.3	157.6
Meats, per man per day,		1.28	$0 18	.15	.48	–
Dairy products and eggs, per man per day,		1.51	11	.08	.15	.05
Animal food, per man per day,		2.79	$0 29	.23	.63	.05
Vegetable food, " "		4.40	10	.21	.04	1.70
Total food, " "		7.19	$0 39	.44	.67	1.75

The figures of this dietary give 98 pounds of fresh meat, costing $14.20, and 17 pounds of salt pork, costing $1.70, or 115 pounds in all, costing $15.90. The explanatory note says that the meat consists of beef (mostly top of sirloin and shoulder clod), about 50 per cent; mutton, 10 per cent; and pork, of which about one-fourth is salt, 40 per cent. This would make the salt pork 10 per cent of the whole meat, whereas the 17 pounds named above would be about 15 per cent. If one-third the pork were salt the statements would coincide. Assuming the percentages to be as above, but allowing the fresh pork to be 25, and the salt 15 per cent, the amounts would be the following, which are assumed for the estimates.

Kind of Meat.	Per cent.	Quantity.
		lbs.
Beef, ...	50	57.7
Mutton, ...	10	11.5
Fresh pork, ...	25	28.8
Totals, ...	85	98.0

The vegetables are said to cost 90 cents and to consist of about 55 per cent of cabbage; 20 per cent, onions; 10 per cent, turnips; and 5 per cent, carrots, the remainder varying according to the season. The following are estimated amounts. The nutrients are computed as in previous cases.

Vegetables.	Per cent.	Quantity.	Price per lb.	Cost.
		lbs.	cts.	
Cabbages, ...	55	36.1	1¼	$0 45
Onions, ...	20	13.1	2	26
Turnips, ...	10	6.6	1	07
Carrots, ...	5	3.3	1	03
Remainder, ...	10	6.6	1¼	09
Totals, ...	100	65.7	–	$0 90

DIETARY NUMBER, B 12.

Description: French Canadian family in Worcester, Mass., consisting of father, mother, and two children, girls of 3 and 5 years, respectively. The father is a printer, and earns $2.00 per day. Time, one month. The demands of the family for nutrients are taken as equivalent to 2.3 men for 30 days, or 1 man for 84 days.

ANALYSIS.

Food-Materials.					Nutrients.		
Kinds.	Prices per lb.	Quanti-ties.	Costs		Protein.	Fats.	(Carbohy-drates.
	cents.	lbs.			lbs.	lbs.	lbs.
Beef, ...	–	24.8			3.3	6.2	–
Beef steak, ...	–	24.7			3.0	9.1	–
Mutton, ...	–	3.3	$10 00		0.5	0.8	–.
Pork, fresh, ...	–	6.6			0.8	2.4	–
Salt pork, ...	–	6.6			0.2	5.0	–
Lard, ...	10	5	‾50		–	5.0	–
Total meats, etc., . . .	. .	71.0	$10 50		7.8	28.5	–
Eggs (9 doz. at 19½ cts.), .	14	12.4	$1 75		1.5	1.3	0.1
Milk (32 qts. at 6¼ cts.), .	3¼	64	2 00		2.2	2.4	3.1
Total dairy products and eggs, ...	. .	76.4	$3 75		3.7	3.7	3.2

DIETARY NUMBER, B 12 — Concluded.

FOOD-MATERIALS.				NUTRIENTS.		
Kinds.	Prices per lb.	Quanti- ties.	Costs.	Protein.	Fats.	Carbohy- drates.
	cents.	lbs.		lbs.	lbs	lbs.
Flour, ...	5	52.0	2 60	5.8	0.6	39.2
Beans (5 qts. at 8 cts), .	4¼	9.4	40	2.3	0.2	5.0
Pease (2 qts. at 7½ cts.), .	⅔	1 9	15	0.4	–	1.0
Rice, ...	–	4.5 }	40	0.3	–	3.6
Barley, ...	–	1.5 }		0.1	–	1.2
Potatoes (1¼ bush.),	¾	75	1 00	1.4	0.2	13.8
Vegetables, . . .	–	36	50	0.4	–	1.9
Apples (½ bush.), . .	1⅔	30	50	0.1	–	3.3
Corn starch, . . .	10	2	20	–	–	1.7
Sugar, ...	8	15	1 20	–	–	14.5
Molasses and syrup (½ gal.), .	3½	5.8	20	–	–	4.1
Raisins and currants, .	15	2	30	0.1	–	1.3
Total vegetable food, . . .		235.1	$7 45	10.9	1.0	90.6
Total animal food, . . .		147.4	14 25	11.5	32.2	3.2
Total food, ...		382.5	$21 70	22 4	33.2	93.8
Meats, etc., per man per day, .		.85	$0 12	.09	.34	–
Dairy products and eggs, per man per day, ...		.91	04	.04	.01	.04
Animal food, per man per day, .		1.76	$0 16	.13	.38	.04
Vegetable food, " "		2.80	09	.13	.01	1.08
Total food, " "		4.56	$0 25	.26	.39	1.12

The meat, stated at 66 pounds, costing $10.00, is said in an explanatory note to consist of about 75 per cent of beef, of which one-half might be rump steak; mutton, 5 per cent; and pork, 20 per cent, one-half of the latter being salt and one-half fresh. The vegetables, stated to cost 50 cents, are estimated to consist of cabbage, 20 per cent; onions, 20 per cent; turnips, 15 per cent; the remainder varying with the season. Vegetables in the quantities and at the prices named would cost 50 cents. These quantities are assumed and the nutrients are estimated as in previous cases.

VEGETABLES.							Per cent.	Quantity.	Price per lb.	Cost.
								lbs.	cts.	
Cabbages, .	.	.	.	.	.	.	20	7½	1¼	$0 10
Onions, .	.	.	.	.	.	.	20	7½	2	15
Turnips, .	.	.	.	.	.	.	15	5	1	05
Remainder,	.	.	.	.	.	.	45	16	1¼	20
Totals, .	.	.	.	.	.	.	100	36	–	$0 50

The mixture of rice and barley, 6 pounds costing 40 cents, is estimated to consist of three-fourths rice and one-fourth barley.

DIETARY NUMBER, B 13.

Description: French Canadian family in Worcester, Mass., consisting of father, mother, and 8 children. Of the latter, 4 are adults, aged 16, 19½, 20, and 25 years, the oldest being a female, and are all mill operatives. The 4 younger children are aged 4, 7, 9, and 13 years. Time, one month. The family are estimated as equivalent in demands for nutrients to 8 men for 30 days, or 1 man for 240 days.

ANALYSIS.

Kinds.	Prices per lb.	Quanti-ties.	Costs.	Protein.	Fats.	Carbohy-drates.
	cents.	lbs.		lbs.	lbs.	lbs.
Beef, ...	–	60 ⎫		7.1	17.9	–
Mutton, ...	–	24 ⎪		3.3	5.6	–
Veal, ...	–	12 ⎬	$18 00	1.8	0.7	–
Pork, fresh, ...	–	6 ⎪		0.7	2.2	–
Pork, salt, ...	–	18 ⎭		0.5	13.8	–
Lard, ...	10	4	40	–	4.0	–
Total meats, etc., . . .	.	124	$18 40	13.4	44.2	–
Eggs (12 doz.), . . .	14½	16.5	$2 40	1.9	1.7	0.1
Butter, ...	25	10	2 50	0.1	8.8	0.1
Milk, ...	3½	136	4 50	4.6	5.0	6.5
Total dairy products and eggs, ...	.	162.5	$9 40	6.6	15.5	6.7
Flour, ...	5	56	$2 80	6.2	0.6	42.2
Rice, ...	–	5.2 ⎫	48	0.4	–	4.1
Barley, ...	–	1.8 ⎬		0.2	–	1.4
Pease (2 qts. at 8 cts.), .	4½	3.8	16	0.9	0.1	2.0
Potatoes (3½ bush.), . .	–	210	3 00	4.0	0.4	38.6
Vegetables, ...	–	74.9	1 24	0.8	0.1	4.8
Corn starch, ...	10	0.5	05	–	–	0.4
Bread (150 two-pound loaves),	2½	300	7 50	26.7	5.7	166.5
Total vegetable food, . .	.	652.2	$15 23	39.2	6.9	260.0
Total animal food, . .	.	286.5	27 89	20.0	59.7	6.7
Total food, . . .	.	938.7	$43 12	59.2	66.6	266.7
Meats, etc., per man per day, .	.	.52	$0 08	.06	.18	–
Dairy products and eggs, per man per day, ...	.	.68	04	.03	.07	.03
Animal food, per man per day,	.	1.20	$0 12	.09	.25	.03
Vegetable food, " " .	.	2.72	06	.16	.03	1.08
Total food, " " .	.	3.92	$0 18	.25	.28	1.11

Of the meat about 50 per cent was beef, usually plate and ribs; 20 per cent, mutton; 10 per cent, veal; and 20 per cent, pork, of which three-fourths was salt.

The figures in the dietary include onions, 3 quarts, costing 24 cents, and other vegetables costing one dollar.

Assuming the remainder to have composition corresponding to onions, which approximates the mean of the whole, and the cost of cabbages, turnips, and carrots to average 1¾ cents per pound, the $1.00 would have bought 70 pounds, of which cabbage would have made 20, turnips 15, carrots 10, and the remainder 25 pounds. The quantities of vegetables would be, therefore, as follows, the quantities being assumed and the nutrients estimated as in previous cases:

VEGETABLES.	Per cent.	Quantity.	Price per lb.	Cost.
		lbs.	cts.	
Onions,	7	4.9	5	$0 24
Cabbages,	27	20		
Turnips,	20	15	} 1 3.7	1 00
Carrots	13	10		
Remainder,	33	25		
Totals,	100	74.9	–	$1 24

Series C. French Canadian, Canada.

The five dietaries of this series which are used in the analyses tables include one of a boarding-house and four of families in Quebec, St. John, Sherbrooke, Richmond, and Rivière du Loup. The averages include, with these, eight others of families and boarding-houses. All are laboring people. The following statements explain dietary habits of the people among whom the statistics were collected.

The meat, aside from salt pork, consists mainly of lamb, veal, and beef, the last being the chief item. The beef is very generally boiled with cabbage. Salt pork is eaten with pea soup. On Fridays the soup only is eaten, the meat being kept until Saturday.

The fish are mostly salt cod, though some salt herring from Labrador are used.

Eggs are estimated to weigh one and a half pounds to the dozen.

Bread, in the province of Quebec, is made by bakers, as a general rule, even in the country. The loaf of ordinary bread has a uniform weight of six pounds, regulated by municipal or provincial law.

Barley is used mainly for soup in a form practically the same as that known in New England and elsewhere as pearled barley.

The vegetables consist ordinarily of cabbage, onions, and carrots. The weight of the cabbages will average six pounds and the price 4 cents per head, making the average price about $\frac{2}{3}$ cents per pound. The onions average $1.20 per bushel of

52 pounds, or $2\frac{1}{3}$ cents per pound.* The carrots usually cost about 40 cents per bushel of 60 pounds, or $\frac{2}{3}$ cents per pound. The three are commonly used in about the proportions by weight of cabbages, 3 pounds; onions, 2 pounds; and carrots, 1 pound.

On the basis of the above data the following estimates have been made:

Meats. For the meat other than salt pork we have assumed for the relative proportions, by weight: Beef, 3; mutton, 1; veal, 1. For the composition of the meat we have considered the fact that the specimens of Chicago beef taken as the basis for computing the composition of beef in the Massachusetts dietaries were fatter than the average of those analyzed in Europe (of which the most are French and German), and presuming that the Canadian beef might approach more nearly to the European averages we have assumed figures for composition approaching nearer to the European standards.

Taking for " moderately fat beef" (flesh free from bone), as its composition: water, 65 per cent; protein, 19 per cent; fats, 14.9 per cent, and mineral matters, 1.1 per cent, and allowing 20 per cent for refuse, bone, etc., we have for beef as purchased, protein 15.2 per cent and fat 11.9 per cent. Taking still further the figures for mutton and veal given in the table on page 261, and allowing the Canadian meat to consist of three parts by weight of beef and one each of mutton and veal, the percentages of nutrients would by a simple computation be protein 14.9, and fats 13.

Vegetables. In estimating the composition of vegetables the data are still less definite. Assuming the vegetables to consist of cabbages, onions, and carrots in the proportions by weight of $3:2:1$; to cost respectively $\frac{2}{3}$ cents, 2 cents, and $\frac{2}{3}$ cents per pound, and to have the composition stated in the

---

* In estimating the composition of vegetables, the cost of onions has been assumed to be, roughly, 2 cents per pound.

table on pages 261 and 262 one dollar would pay for the following quantities:

VEGETABLES.	Quantities.	Costs.	Protein.	Fats.	Carbohy- drates.
	lbs.	cents.	lbs.	lbs	lbs.
Cabbages, ...	45	30	0.76	0.09	1.93
Onions, ...	30	60	0.30	0.06	2 25
Carrots, ...	15	10	0.14	0.03	1.14
Total, for one dollar, . .	90	100	1.20	0.19	5.37

We have accordingly assumed that one dollar would purchase 90 pounds of vegetables, containing 1.2 pounds of protein; 0.2 pounds of fats, and 5.4 pounds of carbohydrates. As the original reports of the dietaries give only the costs of the vegetables, and not the quantities of vegetables and of nutrients in them, we have computed them on this basis. It should be remembered, however, that the quantities of vegetables consumed are small, so that if these estimates vary from the truth the effect upon the general result will be very slight.

As to meats the figures assumed for composition are not far from the mean of meats in common use, and the variations from the truth, wide as they may be, could hardly affect the composition of the dietaries as a whole so materially as to throw great doubt upon the general conclusions derived from comparing them with the dietaries of series A and B.

The figures just explained as taken for estimates of the dietaries of series C are, briefly recapitulated, the following:

FOOD-MATERIALS.	Protein.	Fats.	Carbohydrates.
	Per cent.	Per cent.	Per cent.
"Meat,"	14.9	13.0	–
Salt pork, ...	11.6*	29.9*	–
	lbs.	lbs.	lbs.
Vegetables, for one dollar, ...	1.2	0.2	5.4

* Taken from European analyses.

DIETARY NUMBER, C 1.

Description: Board of 8 adults, working people in Montreal, for one month. Assuming 4 to be males, and 4 to be females, and taking the latter as equal to 3 laboring men, the whole would be equivalent in demands for nutrients to 7 men for 30 days, or 1 man for 210 days.

ANALYSIS.

FOOD-MATERIALS.				NUTRIENTS.		
Kinds.	Prices per lb.	Quanti- ties.	Costs.	Protein.	Fats.	Carbohy- drates.
	cents.	lbs.		lbs.	lbs.	lbs.
Meat, fresh, ...	–	75 }	$10 00	11.2	9.8	–
Salt pork, ...	–	25 }		2.9	7.5	–
Lard, ...	13	10	1 30	–	9.9	–
Total meats, etc., . .	. .	110	$11 30	14.1	27.2	–
Eggs (4 doz. at 15 cts.), . .	10	6	$0 60	0.7	0.6	–
Milk (10 qts. at 5 cts.), . .	2½	20	60	0.7	0.7	1.0
Cheese, ...	10	4	40	1.1	1.4	0.1
Total dairy products and eggs, ...	. .	30	$1 50	2.5	2.7	1.1
Flour, ...	3	28	$0 84	3.1	0.3	21.1
Pease, ...	4	4	16	0.9	0.1	2.1
Beans, ...	7	1	07	0.2	–	0 5
Barley, ...	6	5	30	0.4	–	3.9
Rice, ...	4	3	12	0.2	–	2.4
Potatoes, ...	⅔	120	80	2.3	0.2	22.1
Vegetables, ...	–	90	1 00	1.2	0.2	5.4
Sugar, ...	6	54	3 24	–	–	52.2
Syrup and molasses (2 gals.), .	4	23	90	–	–	16.3
Bread (40 six-pound loaves), .	2⅔	240	6 40	21.4	4.6	133.2
Crackers, ...	10	5.5	55	0.6	0.5	3.8
Total vegetable food, . .	. .	573.5	$14 38	30.3	5.9	263.0
Total animal food, . .	. .	140	12 80	16.6	29.9	1.1
Total food, . . .	. .	713.5	$27 18	46.9	35.8	264.1
Meats, etc., per man per day, .	. .	.52	$0 05	.07	.13	–
Dairy products and eggs, per man per day, ...	. .	.14	01	.01	.01	.01
Animal food, per man per day,	. .	.66	$0 06	.08	.14	.01
Vegetable food, " "	. .	2.73	07	.14	.03	1.25
Total food, " "	. .	3.39	$0 13	.22	.17	1.26

DIETARY NUMBER, C 5.

Description: Family in Montreal, consisting of father, mother, and one child, 3 years old. Time, one month. Assuming the mother to require 0.8, and the child 0.5, as much nutrient as a laboring man, the requirements of the 3 persons may be taken as equivalent in demands for nutrients to 2⅓ laboring men for 30 days, or 1 man for 70 days.

ANALYSIS.

FOOD-MATERIALS.				NUTRIENTS.		
Kinds.	Prices per lb.	Quanti- ties.	Costs.	Protein.	Fats.	Carbohy- drates.
	cents.	lbs.		lbs.	lbs.	lbs.
Meat, ...	–	11.5 }	$2 30	1.7	1.5	–
Salt pork, ...	–	11.5 }		1.3	3.4	–
Lard, ...	13⅓	3	40	–	2.9	–
Salt cod, ·	4	8	32	1.3	–	–
Total meats, fish, etc., .	. .	34	$3 02	4.3	7.8	–

DIETARY NUMBER, C 5 — Concluded.

Kinds.	Price per lb.	Quantities.	Costs.	Protein.	Fats.	Carbohydrates.
FOOD-MATERIALS.				**NUTRIENTS.**		
	cents.	lbs.		lbs.	lbs.	lbs.
Eggs (8 doz., at 15 cts.), . .	10	12	$1 20	1.4	1.2	0.1
Butter, ...	19	17	3 25	0.2	14.8	0.1
Milk (12 qts.), ...	2½	24	60	0.8	0.9	1.2
Total dairy products and eggs, ...	. .	53	$5 05	2.4	16.9	1.4
Flour, ...	3	16.7	$0 50	1.0	0.2	12.6
Rice, ...	4	5	20	0.4	–	4.0
Pease, ...	4	3	12	0.7	0.1	1.6
Beans, ...	7	1	07	0.3	–	0.5
Potatoes, ...	¾	60	40	1.1	0.1	11.0
Vegetables, ...	1 1 9	36	40	–	–	2.2
Corn starch, ...	10	1	10	–	–	0.8
Sugar, ...	6	7	42	–	–	6.8
Syrup and molasses (½ gal.), .	¾	5.8	45	–	–	4.1
Bread (20 six-pound loaves), .	2⅔	120	3 20	10.7	2.3	66.6
Total vegetable food, . .	.	255.5	$5 86	15.1	2.7	110.2
Total animal food, . .	.	87	8 07	6.7	24.7	1.4
Total food, . .	. .	342.5	$13 93	21.8	27.4	111.6
Meats, fish, etc., per man per day, ...		.49	$0 04	.06	.11	–
Dairy products and eggs, per man per day, . . .	.	.75	07	.03	.24	.02
Animal food, per man per day,	.	1.24	$0 11	.09	.35	.02
Vegetable food, " "	.	3.65	08	.22	.04	1.57
Total food, " "	.	4.89	$0 19	.31	.39	1.59

DIETARY NUMBER, C 6.

Description: Family in Quebec, consisting of father, mother, and six children, from 1 to 12 years of age. Time, one month. Assuming one child to be under 2 years, and to require ¼ as much food as a laboring man, two children to be between 3 and 6 years, and to need each ½ as much as a man, and three to be between 6 and 12 years, and to require each 0.7 as much as a man, and allowing for the mother 0.8 the same amount, the family would be equivalent to 5.15, or, in round numbers, 5 men for 30 days, or 1 man for 150 days. This is one of the cases in which this method of computation is particularly unsatisfactory.

ANALYSIS.

Kinds.	Prices per lb.	Quantities.	Costs.	Protein.	Fats.	Carbohydrates.
FOOD-MATERIALS.				**NUTRIENTS.**		
	cents.	lbs.		lbs.	lbs.	lbs.
Meats, ...	–	52.5 }	$7 00	7.8	6.8	–
Salt pork, ...	–	17.5 }		2.0	5.2	–
Salt cod, ...	4	15	60	2.4	0.1	–
Total meats and fish, .	.	85	$7 60	12.2	12.1	–
Eggs (8 doz. at 15 cts.), .	10	12	·$1 20	1.4	1.2	0.1
Butter, ...	18	15	2 70	0.2	13.1	0.1
Milk (60 qts. at 5 cts.), .	2½	120	3 00	4.1	4.4	5.8
Total dairy products and eggs, ...	.	147	$6 90	5.7	18.7	6.0

Dietary Number, C 6 — Concluded.

Food-Materials.				Nutrients.		
Kinds.	Prices per lb.	Quantities.	Costs.	Protein.	Fats.	Carbohydrates.
	cents.	lbs.		lbs.	lbs.	lbs.
Flour,	3	48	$1 44	5.3	0.5	36.2
Rice,	4	8	32	0.6	-	6.3
Barley,	6	7	42	0.6	0.1	5.4
Pease (¼ bush.),	2⅓	15	35	3.4	0.2	7.9
Beans (4 qts at 8 cts.),	4¼	7.5	32	1.7	0.2	4.0
Potatoes (2 bush. at 40 cts.),	⅔	120	80	2.3	0.2	22.1
Vegetables,	-	-	70	0.8	0.1	3 8
Sugar,	7	12	84	-	-	11.6
Bread (20 loaves),	2⅔	120	3 20	10.7	2.3	66.6
Total vegetable food,	. .	337.5	$8 39	25.4	3.6	163.9
Total animal food,	. .	232	14 50	17.9	30.8	6.0
Total food,	. .	569.5	$22 89	43.3	34.4	169.9
Meats and fish, per man per day,	. .	.57	$0 05	.08	.03	-
Dairy products and eggs, per man per day,	. .	.98	05	.04	.12	.04
Animal food, per man per day,	. .	1.55	$0 10	.12	.20	.04
Vegetable food, " "	. .	2.25	06	.17	.02	1.09
Total food, " "	. .	3.80	$0 16	.29	.22	1.13

Dietary Number, C 9.

Description: Family in Quebec, consisting of father, mother, and six children, from 2 to 14 years of age. Time, one month. Assuming two of the children to have been between 2 and 6, and four between 6 and 15 years of age, the whole family would, by the method of estimating here followed, be equivalent in demands for nutrients to 5.1 men. Taking the whole family as equivalent to 5 men, their demand for 30 days would be equal to that of 1 man for 150 days.

ANALYSIS.

Food-Materials.				Nutrients.		
Kinds.	Prices per lb.	Quantities.	Costs.	Protein.	Fats.	Carbohydrates.
	cents.	lbs.		lbs.	lbs.	lbs.
Meat,	-	40 }	$8 00	6.0	5.2	-
Salt pork,	-	40 }		4.6	12.0	-
Salt cod,	4	20	80	3.2	0.1	-
Total meats and fish,	. .	100	$8 80	13.8	17.3	-
Eggs (1½ doz. at 16 cts.),	10⅓	2.3	$0 24	0.3	0.2	-
Milk (8 qts. at 5 cts.),	2½	16	40	0.5	0.6	0.8
Butter,	18	20	3 60	0.2	17.5	0.1
Total dairy products and eggs,	. .	38.3	$4 24	1.0	18.3	0.9
Flour,	3	30	$0 90	3.0	0.3	22.6
Rice,	4	4	16	0.3	-	3.2
Barley,	6	4	24	0.3	-	3.1
Pease (4 qts.),	2⅔	7.5	20	1.7	0.1	3.9
Potatoes (2 bush. at 35 cts.),	⅔	120	70	2.3	0.2	22.1
Vegetables,	-	-	40	0.5	0.1	2.2
Sugar,	6	20	1 20	-	-	19.3
Bread (40 loaves),	2⅔	240	6 40	21.4	4.6	133.2
Total vegetable food,	. .	425.5	$10 20	29.5	5.3	209.6
Total animal food,	. .	138.3	13 04	14.8	35.6	0.9
Total food,	. .	563.8	$23 24	44.3	40.9	210.5

DIETARY NUMBER, C 9 — Concluded.

	FOOD-MATERIALS.			NUTRIENTS.		
Kinds.	Prices per lb.	Quanti- ties.	Costs.	Protein.	Fats.	Carbohy- drates.
	cents.	lbs.		lbs.	lbs.	lbs.
Meats and fish, per man per day, ...	. .	.07	$0 06	.09	.12	–
Dairy products and eggs, per man per day, ...	. .	.26	03	.01	.12	.01
Animal food, per man per day,	. .	.93	$0 09	.10	.24	.01
Vegetable food, " " .	. .	2.84	0 07	.20	.04	1.40
. Total food, " "	. .	3.77	$0 16	.30	.28	1.41

DIETARY NUMBER, C 11.

Description: Family in St. John, consisting of father, mother, and three children from 2 to 7 years of age. Time, one month. Assuming one child to be between 6 and 15, and two to be between 2 and 6 years of age, the whole family would, by the method of estimating here followed, be equivalent in demands for nutrients to 3.5 men for 30 days, or to 1 man for 105 days.

ANALYSIS.

	FOOD-MATERIALS.			NUTRIENTS.		
Kinds.	Prices per lb.	Quanti- ties.	Costs.	Protein.	Fats.	Carbohy- drates.
	cents.	lbs.		lbs.	lbs.	lbs.
Meat, ...	–	30 ⎱	$4 00	4.5	3.9	–
Salt pork, ...	–	10 ⎰		1.2	3.0	–
Lard, ...	15	5	75	–	4.9	–
Salt cod, ...	4	10	40	0.2	0.1	–
Total meats, fish, etc., .	. .	55	$5 15	5.9	11.9	–
Eggs (8 doz.), ...	10	12	$1 20	1.3	0.1	0 1
Butter, ...	18	10	1 80	0.7	8.8	0.1
Milk, ...	2½	72	1 80	2.3	2.7	3.5
Total dairy products and eggs, ...	. .	94	$4 80	3.7	11.6	3.7
Flour, ...	3	33	$1 00	3.7	0.4	24.9
Rice, ...	4	6	24	0.4	–	4.8
Pease, ...	4	7	28	1.6	0.1	3.7
Beans, ...	7	2	14	0.5	–	1.1
Potatoes, ...	½	60	35	1.1	0.1	11.0
Vegetables, ...	1 1-9	27	30	0.4	0.1	1.6
Sugar, ...	6	12	72	–	–	11.6
Syrup and molasses (1 gal.), .	3½	11.5	40	–	–	8.2
Bread, ...	2⅞	114	3 04	10.1	2.2	63.3
Total vegetable food, . .	. .	272.5	$6 47	17.8	2.9	130.2
Total animal food, . .	. .	149	9 95	9.6	23.5	3.7
Total food, . . .	. .	421.5	$16 42	27.4	26.4	133.9
Meats, fish, etc., per man per day, ...	. .	.52	$0 05	.06	.11	–
Dairy products and eggs, per man per day, ...	. .	.90	05	.04	.11	.04
Animal food, per man per day,	. .	1.42	$0 10	.10	.22	.04
Vegetable food, " "	. .	2.59	06	.17	.03	1.24
Total food, " "	. .	4.01	$0 16	.27	.25	1.28

Dietary Number, C 12.

Description: Family in St. John, consisting of father, mother, and eight children from 2 to 13 years of age. Time, one month. Assuming five of the children to have been between 6 and 12, and three between 2 and 6 years of age, the whole family would, by the method of estimating before explained, be equivalent in demands for nutrients to 6.8 men. Taking the demand at 6⅔ men for 30 days, it would be equivalent to 1 man for 200 days.

ANALYSIS.

Kinds.	Prices per lb.	Quantities.	Costs.	Protein.	Fats.	Carbohydrates.
	cents.	lbs.		lbs.	lbs.	lbs.
Meat, ...	-	22.5 }	$4 50	3.4	2.9	-
Salt pork, ...	-	22.5 }		2.6	6 7	-
Lard, ...	13	4	52	-	4.0	-
Salt cod, ...	4	20	80	3.2	0.1	-
Total meats, fish, etc., . .	. .	69.0	$5 82	9.2	13.7	-
Eggs (4 doz. at 16 cts.), . .	10⅔	6	$0 64	0.7	0 6	-
Milk (30 qts. at 5 cts.), . .	2½	60	1 50	2.0	2.2	2.9
Butter, ...	18	22	4 00	0.2	19.3	0.1
Total dairy products and eggs, ...	. .	88	$6 14	2.9	22.1	3.0
Flour, ...	3	20	$0 60	2.2	0.2	15.1
Rice, ...	4	7	28	0.5	-	5.5
Pease, ...	4	8	32	1.8	0.1	4.2
Beans, ...	7	1	07	0.2	-	0.5
Potatoes (2 bush.), . .	3-5	120	75	2.3	0.2	22.1
Vegetables, . . .	1 1-9	22.5	25	0.3	-	1.4
Sugar, ...	6	17	1 00	-	-	16.4
Syrup and molasses (2½ gals.),	3½	28.8	1 00	-	-	20.4
Bread (30 loaves), . .	2⅔	180	4 80	16.0	3.5	99.9
Total vegetable food, . .	. .	404.3	$0 07	23.3	4.0	185 5
Total animal food, . .	. .	157	11 96	12.1	35.8	3.0
Total food, . . .	. .	561.3	$21 03	35.4	39.8	188.5
Meats, fish, etc., per man per day, ...	. .	.35	$0 03	.05	.07	-
Dairy products and eggs, per man per day, . .	. .	.44	03	.01	.11	.02
Animal food, per man per day,	. .	.79	$0 06	.06	.18	.02
Vegetable food, " " .	. .	2.02	05	.12	.02	.93
Total food, " " .	. .	2.81	$0 11	.18	.20	.95

Dietary Number, C 13.

Description: Board of 10 adults in Sorel, for one month. Assuming five to have been females equivalent to four men, the whole would be equivalent in demands for nutrients to 9 men for 30 days, or 1 man for 270 days.

ANALYSIS.

Kinds.	Prices per lb	Quantities.	Costs.	Protein.	Fats.	Carbohydrates.
	cents.	lbs.		lbs.	lbs.	lbs.
Meat, fresh, ...	-	47.5 }	$9 50	7.1	6.2	-
Pork, salt, ...	-	47.5 }		5.5	14.1	-
Lard, ...	-	14	1 80	-	13.9	-
Total meats, etc., . .	. .	109.0	$11 30	12.6	34.2	-

DIETARY NUMBER, C 13 — Concluded.

Kinds.	Prices per lb.	Quanti-ties.	Costs.	Protein.	Fats.	Carbohy-drates.
	cents.	lbs.		lbs.	lbs.	lbs.
Eggs (3 doz. at 15 cts.),	10	4.5	$0 45	5.2	0.5	–
Milk (15 qts. at 5 cts.),	–	30	75	1.0	1.1	1.4
Cheese,	–	4	40	1.1	1.4	0.1
Total dairy products and eggs,		38.5	$1 60	7.3	3.0	1.5
Flour,	3	35	$1 05	3.9	0.4	26.4
Pease,	4	5	20	1.1	0.1	2.6
Beans,	7	3	21	0.7	0.1	1.6
Barley,	6	7	42	0.6	–	5.4
Rice,	4	2	08	0.1	–	1.6
Potatoes (3 bush.),	¾	180	1 20	3.4	0.4	33.1
Vegetables,	–	–	1 50	1.8	0.3	8.1
Apples (1 bush.),	–	60	1 00	0.2	–	6.5
Corn starch,	10	1	10	–	–	0.8
Sugar,	6	35	2 10	–	–	33.8
Molasses and syrup (7 gals.),	–	80.5	3 15	–	–	57.2
Bread (36¼ six-pound loaves),	2¾	217.5	5 80	19.4	4.1	120.7
Crackers,	10	5	50	0.5	0.5	3.4
Total vegetable food,		631	$17 31	31.7	5.9	301.2
Total animal food,		147.5	12 90	19.9	37.2	1.5
Total food,		778.5	$30 21	51.6	43.1	302.7
Meats, etc., per man per day,		.40	$0 04	.05	.13	–
Dairy products and eggs, per man per day,		.14	01	.03	.01	.01
Animal food, per man per day,		.54	$0 05	.08	.14	.01
Vegetable food, " "		2.34	06	.12	.02	1.12
Total food, " "		2.88	$0 11	.20	.16	1.13

DIETARY NUMBER, C 14.

Description: Board of 12 adults in Sorel. Time, one month. Assuming six to have been females, their requirements for nutrients would, by the method of estimating here followed, have been equal to that of about 5 (4.8) men, making the whole equivalent to 11 men for 30 days, or 1 man for 330 days.

ANALYSIS.

Kinds.	Prices per lb.	Quanti-ties.	Costs.	Protein.	Fats.	Carbohy-drates.
	cents.	lbs.		lbs.	lbs.	lbs.
Meat, fresh,	–	47.5 }	$9 50	7.1	6.2	–
Salt pork,	–	47.5 }		5.5	14.2	–
Lard,	13	6	78	–	6.0	–
Fish, salt cod,	5	30	1 50	4.8	0.1	–
Total meats, fish, etc.,		131	$11 78	17.4	26.5	–
Eggs (11 doz., at 15 cts.),	10	16.5	$1 65	1.9	1.7	0.1
Milk (20 qts., at 5 cts.),	–	40	1 00	1.4	1.5	1.9
Cheese,	10	9	90	2.4	3.2	0.2
Butter,	18	25	4 50	0.2	21.9	0.1
Total dairy products and eggs,		90.5	$8 05	5.9	28.3	2.3

DIETARY NUMBER, C 14 — Concluded.

FOOD-MATERIALS.				NUTRIENTS.		
Kinds.	Prices per lb.	Quanti- ties.	Costs.	Protein.	Fats.	Carbohy- drates.
	cents.	lbs.		lbs.	lbs.	lbs.
Flour, ...	3	53.3	$1 60	5.9	0.6	40.2
Pease, ...	4	10	40	2.3	0.2	5.2
Beans, ...	7	3	21	0.7	0.1	1.6
Barley, ...	6	5	30	0.4	–	3.9
Rice, ...	4	2	08	0.1	–	1.6
Potatoes, (2 bush.), . .	⅔	120	80	2.3	0.2	22.1
Vegetables, . . .	1 1.0	135	1 50	1.8	0.3	8.1
Apples (1½ bush.), . .	–	90	1 50	0.3	–	9.8
Corn starch, ...	10	2	20	–	–	1.7
Sugar, ...	6	23.5	1 40	–	–	22.7
Syrup and molasses (7 gals.), .	–	80.5	3 60	–	–	57.2
Bread (50 six-pound loaves), .	2⅔	300	8 00	26.7	5.7	166.5
Total vegetable food, . .	. .	824.3	$19 99	40.5	7.1	340.6
Total animal food, . .	. .	221.5	19 83	23.3	54.8	2.3
Total food, . . .	. .	1,045.8	$38 82	63.8	61.9	342.9
Meats, fish, etc., per man per day, ...	. .	.40	$0 04	.05	.08	–
Dairy products and eggs, per man per day, ...	. .	.27	02	.02	.09	.01
Animal food, per man per day,	. .	.67	$0 06	.07	.17	.01
Vegetable food, " "	. .	2.50	06	.12	.02	1.03
Total food, " "	. .	3.17	$0 12	.19	.19	1.04

DIETARY NUMBER, C 18.

Description: Board of 15 adults, in Rivière du Loup. Time, one month. Assuming eight of the persons to have been men and seven, women, the latter would, on the basis of calculation here used, be equivalent in demands for nutrients to 5.6 men, and the whole to 13.6 men, or 13½ men for 30 days would be equivalent to 1 man for 405 days.

ANALYSIS.

FOOD-MATERIALS.				NUTRIENTS.		
Kinds.	Prices per lb.	Quanti- ties.	Costs.	Protein.	Fats.	Carbohy- drates.
	cents.	lbs.		lbs.	lbs.	lbs.
Meat, fresh, ...	10	125	$12 50	18.6	16.3	–
Lard, ...	13	20	2 60	–	19.8	–
Total meats, etc., . .	. .	145	$15 10	18.6	36.1	–
Eggs (4 doz. at 15 cts.), . .	10	6	$0 60	0.7	0.6	–
Milk (16 qts.), ...	2½	32	80	1.1	1.2	1.5
Butter, ...	18	35	6 30	0.4	30.6	0.2
Cheese, ...	10	5	50	1.4	1.8	0.1
Total dairy products and eggs, ...	. .	78	$8 20	3.6	34.2	1.8
Flour, ...	8	35	$1 05	3.9	0.4	26.4
Rice, ...	4	3	12	0.2	–	2.4
Barley, ...	6	4	24	0.3	–	3.1
Pease, ...	4	7	29	1.6	0.1	3.7
Beans, ...	7	2	14	0.5	–	1.2
Potatoes (3 bush., at 40 cts.), .	⅔	180	1 20	3.4	0.4	33.1
Vegetables, ...	–	–	1 00	1.2	0.2	5.4
Sugar, ...	6	60	3 60	–	–	58.0
Syrup and molasses (1 gal.), .	4½	11.5	50	–	–	8.2

Dietary Number, C 18 — Concluded.

	FOOD-MATERIALS.			NUTRIENTS.		
Kinds.	Prices per lb.	Quanti-ties.	Costs.	Protein.	Fats.	Carbohy-drates.
	cents.	lbs.		lbs.	lbs.	lbs.
Bread, ...	2⅔	360	$9 60	32.0	6.8	109.8
Crackers, ...	10	7	70	0.7	0.7	4.8
Total vegetable food, . .		669.5	$18 43	43.8	8.6	340.1
Total animal food, . .		223	23 30	22.2	70.3	1.8
Total food, . . .		892.5	$41 73	66.0	78.9	347.9
Meats, etc., per man per day, .		.36	$0 04	.04	.09	–
Dairy products and eggs, per man per day, ...		.19	02	.01	.08	
Animal food, per man per day,		.55	$0 06	.05	.17	–
Vegetable food, " " .		1.65	05	.11	.02	.85
Total food, " " .		2.20	$0 11	.16	.19	.85

Dietary Number, C 21.

Description: Family in St. Hyacinth, consisting of father, mother, and four children from 2 to 9 or 10 years of age. Time, one month. Assuming two of the children to be between 2 and 6, and two to be between 6 and 15 years, the whole family would, as here computed, be equivalent in food requirements to 4.2 men for 30 days, or 1 man for 126 days.

ANALYSIS.

	FOOD-MATERIALS.			NUTRIENTS.		
Kinds.	Prices per lb.	Quanti-ties.	Costs.	Protein.	Fats.	Carbohy-drates.
	cents.	lbs.		lbs.	lbs.	lbs.
Meat, ...	–	30 ⎫		4 5	3.9	–
Ham, ...	–	5 ⎬	$4 00	0.7	1.7	–
Salt pork, ...	–	5 ⎭		0.6	1.5	–
Salt fish (cod), . . .	4	10	40	1 6	–	–
Total meats and fish, .		50	$4 40	7.4	7.1	–
Eggs (4 doz. at 15 cts.), .	10	6	$0 60	0.7	0.6	–
Milk (26 qts. at 5 cts.), .	2¼	32	80	1.1	1.2	1.5
Butter, ...	18	12	2 16	0.1	10.5	0.1
Total dairy products and eggs, ...		50	$3 56	1.9	12.3	1.6
Flour, ...	3	12	$0 36	1.3	0.1	9.1
Rice, ...	–	3 ⎫	30	0.2	–	2.4
Barley, ...	–	3 ⎭		0.3	–	2.3
Pease (4 qts.), . . .	2⅔	7.5	20	1.7	0.1	3.9
Potatoes (1 bush.), . .	⅞	60	35	1.1	0.1	11.0
Vegetables, . . .	1 1.9	45	50	0.6	0.1	2.7
Sugar, ...	6	12	72	–	–	11.6
Syrup and molasses (1 qt.),	⅞	2.9	25	–	–	2 1
Bread (25 loaves), . .	2⅔	150	4 00	13.4	2.9	83 3
Total vegetable food, .		295.4	$6 68	18.6	3.3	128.4
Total animal food, .		100	7 96	9.3	19.4	1.6
Total food, . . .		395.4	$14 64	27.9	22.7	130.0
Meats and fish, per man per day, ...		.40	$0 04	.06	.06	–
Dairy products and eggs, per man per day, . . .		.40	03	.02	.10	.01
Animal food, per man per day,		.80	$0 07	.08	.16	.01
Vegetable food, " "		2.34	05	.15	.03	1.02
Total food, " " .		3.14	$0 12	.23	.19	1.03

DIETARY NUMBER, C 24.

Description: Family in Sherbrooke, consisting of father, mother, and two children, one of 5 years and one of 6 mouths. Time, one month. The family are computed as equivalent in their demands for nutrients to 2½ men for 30 days, or 1 man for 75 days.

ANALYSIS.

	FOOD-MATERIALS.			NUTRIENTS.		
Kinds.	Prices per lb.	Quanti-ties.	Costs.	Protein.	Fats.	Carbohy-drates.
	cents.	lbs.		lbs	lbs.	lbs.
Meat, fresh, ...	–	30 ⎰	$6 00	4.5	3.9	–
Salt pork, ...	–	30 ⎱		3.5	9.0	–
Salt fish (cod), . . .	–	25	1 00	2.8	0.1	–
Total meats and fish, . . .	. .	85	$7 00	10.8	13.0	–
Eggs (2 doz. at 15 cts.), . .	10	3	$0 30	0.3	0.3	–
Milk (12 qts.), ...	–	24	62	0.8	0.9	1.2
Cheese, ...	10	2	20	0.5	0.7	–
Butter, ...	18	12	2 16	0.1	10.5	0.1
Total dairy products and eggs, ...	. .	41	$3 28	1.7	12.4	1.3
Flour, ...	3	6	$0 18	0.7	0.1	4.5
Pease, ...	4	4	16	0.9	0.1	2.1
Beans, ...	–	4	30	0.9	0.1	2.1
Barley, ...	6	3	18	0.3	–	2.3
Rice, ...	4	2	08	0.1	–	1.6
Potatoes (1 bush.), . .	⅔	60	40	1.1	0.1	11.0
Vegetables, ...	–	–	30	0.4	0.1	1.8
Sugar, ...	6	8	48	–	–	7.7
Syrup and molasses (1½ gal.), .	4	5.7	30	–	–	4.0
Bread (15 six-pound loaves), .	2⅔	90	2 40	8.0	1.7	50.0
Total vegetable food, . .	. .	182.7	$4 63	12.4	2.2	87.1
Total animal food, . .	. .	126	10 23	12.5	25.4	1.3
Total food, ...	. .	308.7	$14 96	24.9	27.6	89.4
Meats and fish, per man per day, ...	. .	1.13	$0 09	.14	.17	–
Dairy products and eggs, per man per day, ...		.55	04	.02	.17	.02
Animal food, per man per day,	. .	1.68	$0 13	.16	.34	.02
Vegetable food, " "	. .	2.43	06	.17	.03	1.16
Total food, " "	. .	4.11	$0 19	.33	.37	1.18

DIETARY NUMBER, C 25.

Description: Family in Richmond, consisting of father, mother, and six children from 2 to 13 years. Time, one month. Assuming two of the children to be between 2 and 6, and four between 6 and 15 years of age, and one of the adult children to be male and the other female, the whole family may be estimated as equivalent in demands for nutrients to 7½ men. These for 30 days would be equivalent to 1 man for 225 days. This is another case in which the lack of definite data makes the estimate somewhat unsatisfactory.

ANALYSIS.

	FOOD-MATERIALS.			NUTRIENTS.		
Kinds.	Prices per lb.	Quanti-ties.	Costs.	Protein.	Fats.	Carbohy-drates.
	cents.	lbs.		lbs.	lbs.	lbs.
Meat, ...	–	31 ⎰	$6 20	3.6	9.3	–
Salt pork, ...	–	31 ⎱		4.6	4.0	–
Lard, ...	13	8	1 04	–	7.9	–
Salt fish (cod), . . .	4	25	1 00	4.0	0.1	–
Total meats, fish, etc., .	. .	95	$8 24	12.2	21.3	–

Dietary Number, C 25 — Concluded.

	FOOD-MATERIALS			NUTRIENTS.		
Kinds.	Prices per lb.	Quanti-ties.	Costs.	Protein.	Fats.	Carbohy-drates.
	cents.	lbs.		lbs.	lbs.	lbs.
Eggs (6 doz. at 15 cts.),	10	9	$0 90	1.0	0.9	0.1
Butter,	18	20	3 60	0.2	17.5	0.1
Cheese,	10	3	30	0.8	1.1	0.1
Milk (24 qts. at 5 cts.)	2½	48	1 20	1.6	1.8	2.3
Total dairy products and eggs,		80	$6 00	3.6	21.3	2.6
Flour,	3	13.3	$0 40	1.5	0.2	10.0
Rice,	4	15	60	1.1	0.1	11.9
Pease,	4	6	24	1.4	0.1	3.1
Potatoes,	⅔	180	1 25	3.4	0.4	33.1
Vegetables,	1 1-9	8.1	90	1.1	0.2	4.9
Sugar,	6	40	2 40	-	-	38.7
Syrup and molasses (3 gals.),	3⅗	34.5	1 26	-	-	24.5
Bread,	2⅔	195	5 20	17.4	3.7	108.2
Total vegetable food,		491.9	$12 25	25.9	4.7	234.4
Total animal food,		175	14 24	15.8	42.6	2 6
Total food,		666.9	$26 49	41.7	47.3	237.0
Meats, fish, etc., per man per day,		.42	$0 04	.05	.09	-
Dairy products and eggs, per man per day,		.36	03	.02	.09	.01
Animal food, per man per day,		.78	$0 07	.07	.18	.01
Vegetable food, " "		2.19	05	.12	.02	1.04
Total food, " "		2.97	$0 12	.19	.20	1.05

Dietary Number, C 26.

Description : Family in Richmond, consisting of father, mother, and three children respectively 9, 12, and 14 years. Time, one month. By the method of computation here followed, the whole family would be equivalent in demands for nutrients to about 4 (3.9) men for 30 days, or 1 man for 120 days.

ANALYSIS.

	FOOD-MATERIALS.			NUTRIENTS.		
Kinds.	Prices per lb.	Quanti-ties.	Costs.	Protein.	Fats.	Carbohy drates.
	cents.	lbs.		lbs.	lbs.	lbs.
Meat,	10	52	$5 20	7.8	0.8	-
Lard,	13½	4.5	60	-	4.5	-
Salt cod,	4	18.8	75	3.0	0.1	-
Total meats, fish, etc.,		75.3	$6 55	10.8	11.4	-
Eggs (4½ doz. at 15 cts.),	10	6 4	$0 64	0.7	0 7	-
Butter,	18	11	2 00	0.1	9.6	0.1
Milk,	2½	36	90	1.2	1.3	1.7
Total dairy products and eggs,		53.4	$3 54	2.0	11.6	1 8
Flour,	3	16	$0 48	1.8	0.2	12.0
Rice,	4	4	16	0.3	-	3.2
Pease,	4	5	20	1.1	0.1	2.6
Beans,	7	2	14	0.5	-	1.2
Potatoes,	⅔	90	60	1.7	0.2	16.6
Vegetables,	1 1-9	72	80	1.0	0.2	4.3
Sugar,	6	18.7	1 12	-	-	18.1
Syrup and molasses (3 gals. at 40 cts.),	3½	34.5	1 20	-	-	24.5
Bread,	2⅔	96	2 56	8.5	1.8	53.3
Total vegetable food,		338.2	$7 26	14.9	2.5	135 8
Total animal food,		128.7	10 09	12.8	23.0	1.8
Total food,		466.9	$17 35	27.7	25.6	137.6

DIETARY NUMBER, C 26 — Concluded.

Food-Materials.				Nutrients.		
Kinds.	Prices per lb.	Quanti-ties.	Costs.	Protein.	Fats.	Carbohy-drates.
	cents.	lbs.		lbs.	lbs.	lbs.
Meats, fish, etc., per man per day, ...	. .	.63	$0 05	.09	.10	–
Dairy products and eggs, per man per day, ...	. .	.45	03	.02	.10	.02
Animal food, per man per day,	. .	1.08	$0 08	.11	.20	.02
Vegetable food, " " .	. .	2.82	07	.12	.02	1.13
Total food, " " .	. .	3.90	$0 15	.23	.22	1.15

Persons stated to be Nourished by Food of Dietaries, and Estimated Numbers of "Laboring Men at Moderate Work" who would require the same Quantities of Nutrients.

Number of dietary.	Persons Reported.	Classification.					Total number of persons.	Esti-mated equiva-lent to laboring men.
		Adults.		Children.				
		Males.	Females.	15 to 6 years.	6 to 2 years.	Under 2 years.		
	Miscellaneous, Massachu-setts.							
A 11	Father, mother, one other adult female, 3 children of 5, 11, and 12 years.	1	2	2	1	–	6	4½
A 1	Boarding-house, 66 males and 11 females.	66	11	–	–	–	77	75
A 7	Boarding-house, 20 males and 16 females.	20	16	–	–	–	36	33
A 2	Boarding-house, 10 males and 60 females.	10	60	–	–	–	70	58
A 9	Husband and wife.	1	1	–	–	–	2	1 4-5
	French Canadian, Mas-sachusetts.							
B 0	Father, mother, 2 adult children,* and 2 chil-dren of 9 and 12½ years.	2	2	2	–	–	6	5
B 4	Boarding-house, 8 men, 7 women, and 3 children.	8	7	3	–	–	18	15½
B 1	Father, mother and 4 adult children, one fe-male.	4	2	–	–	–	6	5½
B 5	Boarding-house, 6 males and 4 females, ages 16–40 years.	6	4	–	–	–	10	9½
B 10	Two brothers and a sis-ter, adults.	2	1	–	–	–	3	3
	French Canadian, Can-ada.							
C 18	Boarding-house, 15 adults.	8	7	–	–	–	15	13½
C 12	Father, mother, and 8 children, 2 to 13 years old.	1	1	5	3	–	10	6⅔
C 26	Father, mother, and 3 children of 9, 12, and 14 years.	1	1	3	–	–	5	4
C 24	Father, mother, and 2 children, 6 months and 5 years old.	1	1	–	1	1	4	2½
C 6	Father, mother, and 6 children, 1 to 12 years old.	1	1	3	2	1	8	5

* One male and one female.

STATEMENTS OF RESULTS.

The table on page 305 is sufficiently explained by its title and by the statements made on pages 266–268, *ante*. It is intended to show the data and results of the estimates of the number of average "laboring men at moderate work" who would be equivalent in requirements of nutritive material to the persons stated to be actually nourished by the food of

Recapitulation of Analyses of Dietaries. Persons,

		PERSONS, EMPLOYMENTS, WAGES, ETC.							
		Adults.				Wages per day.		Board per week.	
Number of dietary.	DIETARIES.	Males.	Females.	Children.	OCCUPATIONS.	Males.	Females.	Males.	Females.
	Miscellaneous, Mass.								
A 11	Family, E. Cambridge.	1	2	3	Father, glass-blower, work exhausting.	$4 00[1]	–	–	–
A 1	Boarding-house, Lowell.	66	11	–	Mill operatives.	–	–	–	–
A 7	Boarding-house, Lynn.	20	16	–	Operatives,[2] dress-makers, clerks.	–	–	–	–
A 2	Boarding-house, Lowell.	10	60	–	Mill operatives.	–	–	–	–
A 9	Family, Boston.	1	1	–	Husband, machinist.	3 25[3]	–	–	–
	Average of 7 diet-aries.								
	French Canadian, Mass.								
B 6	Family, Holyoke.	2	2	2	Mill operatives.	1 35	$0 90	–	–
B 4	Boarding-house, Holyoke.	8	7	3	" "	1 25	90	2 75	2 00
B 1	Family, Lawrence.	4	2	–	" "	_4	90	–	–
B 5	Boarding-house, Holyoke.	6	4	–	" "	_5	_6	–	–
B 10	Family, Lowell.	2	1	–	Men, blacksmiths; woman, mill operative.	2 00[7]	1 00	–	–
	Average of 10 diet-aries.								
	French Canadian, Canada.								
C 18	Boarding-house, Rivière du Loup.	15		–	⎫	–	–	–	–
C 12	Family, St. John.	1	1	8	⎪ All laboring peo-ple.	–	–	–	–
C 26	Family, Richmond.	1	1	3	⎬	–	–	–	–
C 24	Family, Sherbrooke.	1	1	2	⎪	–	–	–	–
C 6	Family, Quebec.	1	1	6	⎭	–	–	–	–
	Average of 13 diet-aries.								

[1] $24.00 per week.　　　　[2] In shoe factories.　　　　[3] $19.50 per week.
[4] $1.25 to $1.75 per day.　[5] $1.25 to $1.50 per day.　[6] 90 cents to $1.00 per day.
[7] $600 per year.

each dietary. Except in the cases in which the sex of the adults and the ages of the children are not stated and must be assumed, the estimates seem to be reasonably close to the truth.

The two tables on pages 306–309 recapitulate the analyses of the dietaries, as estimated per man per day.

The table on page 310 summarizes in shorter form the principal results set forth in the three tables preceding.

Employments, Wages, etc., and Quantities and Costs of Food.

FOOD-MATERIALS PER MAN PER DAY.										
QUANTITIES.					COSTS.					
Animal food.					Animal food.					
Meats, fish, etc.	Dairy products and eggs.	Total.	Vegetable food.	Total food.	Meats, fish, etc.	Dairy products and eggs.	Total.	Vegetable food.	Total food.	Number of dietary.
lbs.	lbs.	lbs.	lbs.	lbs.	cts.	cts.	cts.	cts.	cts.	
.66	.82	1.48	2.97	4.45	9	7	16	9	25	A 11
.90	1.55	2.54	2.65	5.19	9	6	15	7	22	A 1
.71	.91	1.62	3.48	5.10	10	5	15	9	24	A 7
.98	1.29	2.27	2.66	4.93	10	5	15	7	22	A 2
1.36	1.64	3.00	4.17	7.17	24	12	36	11	47	A 9
.88	1.29	2.17	3.02	5.19	11	6	17	8	25	
.46	.21	.67	2.35	3.02	7	3	10	7	17	B 6
.95	.80	1.75	2.76	4.51	12	6	18	6	24	B 4
.92	.66	1.58	3.01	4.59	14	4	18	9	27	B 1
1.05	.39	1.44	4.25	5.69	14	5	19	9	28	B 5
1.28	1.51	2.79	4.40	7.19	18	11	29	10	39	B 10
.81	.70	1.51	3.44	4.95	11	5	16	8	24	
.36	.19	.55	1.65	2.20	4	2	6	5	11	C 18
.35	.44	.79	2.02	2.81	3	3	6	5	11	C 12
.63	.45	1.08	2.82	3.90	5	3	8	7	15	C 26
1.13	.55	1.68	2.43	4.11	9	4	13	6	19	C 24
.57	.98	1.55	2.25	3.80	5	5	10	6	16	C 0
.52	.45	.97	2.49	3.46	5	3	8	6	14	

Recapitulation of Analyses of Dietaries.

Number of dietary.	DIETARIES.	NUTRIENTS SUPPLIED BY DIFFERENT CLASSES OF FOOD-MATERIALS.									
		PROTEIN.				FATS.				CARBOHYDRATES.	
		Animal food.			Vegetable food.	Animal food.			Vegetable food.	Dairy products and eggs.	Vegetable food.
		Meats, fish, etc.	Dairy products and eggs.	Total.		Meats, fish, etc.	Dairy products and eggs.	Total.			
		lbs.	lbs.	lbs.	lbs.	lbs.	lbs.	lbs.	lbs.	lbs.	lbs.
	Miscellaneous, Massachusetts.										
A 11	Family, East Cambridge.	.07	.03	.10	.11	.13	.14	.27	.02	.03	1.03
A 1	Boarding-house, Lowell.	.11	.06	.17	.12	.31	.18	.49	.01	.07	1.13
A 7	Boarding-house, Lynn.	.09	.04	.13	.12	.19	.12	.31	.02	.04	1.11
A 2	Boarding-house, Lowell.	.11	.05	.16	.13	30	.13	.43	.01	.06	1.15
A 9	Family, Boston.	.17	.08	.25	.15	.31	.21	.52	.04	.07	1.29
	Average of 7 dietaries.	.11	.05	.16	.12	.24	.15	.39	.02	.06	1.11
	French Canadians, Massachusetts.										
B 6	Family, Holyoke.	.04	.02	.06	.12	.21	.06	.27	.02	–	1.09
B 4	Boarding-house, Holyoke.	.09	.04	.13	.08	.49	.09	.58	.01	.03	.60
B 1	Family, Lawrence.	.10	.03	.13	.12	.33	.07	.40	.01	.03	1.12
B 5	Boarding-house, Holyoke.	.10	.02	.12	.10	.47	.10	.57	.02	.01	1.21
B 10	Family, Lowell.	.15	.08	.23	.21	.48	.15	.63	.04	.05	1.70
	Average of 10 dietaries.	.08	.04	.12	.14	.34	.09	.43	.02	.02	1.19
	French Canadians, Canada.										
C 18	Boarding-house, Rivière du Loup.	.04	.01	.05	.11	.09	.08	.17	.02	–	.85
C 12	Family, St. John.	.05	.01	.06	.12	.07	.11	.18	.02	.02	.93
C 26	Family, Richmond.	.09	.02	.11	.12	.10	.10	.20	.02	.02	1.13
C 24	Family, Sherbrooke.	.14	.02	.16	.17	.17	.17	.34	.03	.02	1 16
C 6	Family, Quebec.	.08	.04	.12	17	.08	.12	.20	.02	.04	1.09
	Average of 13 dietaries.	.07	.02	.09	.15	.10	.11	.21	.03	.02	1.14

Quantities of Nutrients Estimated per Man per Day.

TOTAL NUTRIENTS SUPPLIED.						Of every 100 parts of protein the different classes of food-materials furnish parts as below.				Number of dietary.
Hundredths of a pound.			Grams.			Animal food.			Vegetable food.	
Protein.	Fats.	Carbohydrates.	Protein.	Fats.	Carbohydrates.	Meats, fish, etc.	Dairy products and eggs.	Total.	Vegetable food.	
lbs.	lbs.	lbs.	grams.	grams.	grams.	per cent.	per cent.	per cent.	per cent.	
.21	.29	1.06	95	132	481	33	14	47	53	A 11
.29	.50	1.20	132	227	545	38	21	59	41	A 1
.25	.33	1.15	114	150	522	36	16	52	48	A 7
.29	.44	1.21	132	200	549	38	17	55	45	A 2
.40	.56	1.36	182	254	617	42	20	62	38	A 9
.28	.41	1.17	127	186	531	39)	18	57	43	
.18	.29	1.09	82	132	495	22	11	33	67	B 6
.21	.59	.72	95	268	327	43	19	62	38	B 4
.25	.41	1.15	114	186	523	40	12	52	48	B 1
.31	.59	1.22	141	268	554	32	7	39	61	B 5
.44	.67	1.75	200	304	795	34	18	52	48	B 10
.26	.45	1.21	118	204	549	31	15	46	54	
.16	.19	.85	73	86	386	25	6	31	69	C 18
.18	.20	.95	82	91	431	28	5	33	67	C 12
.23	.22	1.15	104	100	522	39	9	48	52	C 26
.33	.37	1.18	150	168	536	42	6	48	52	C 24
.29	.22	1.13	132	100	513	27	14	41	59	C 6
.24	.24	1.16	109	109	527	29	8	37	63	

*Summary of Analyses of Dietaries. Quantities and Costs of Foods and Quantities of Nutrients. Maximum, Minimum, and Average per Man per Day.**

QUANTITIES, COSTS, AND NUTRIENTS OF FOOD-MATERIALS.	A. Miscellaneous, Massachusetts.			B. French Canadian, Massachusetts.			C. French Canadian, Canada.		
	Maximum.	Minimum.	Average.	Maximum.	Minimum.	Average.	Maximum.	Minimum.	Average.
Quantities of Food-Materials.	lbs.	lbs.	lbs.	lbs.	lbs.	lbs.	lbs.	lbs.	lbs.
Meats, fish, etc., . .	1.36	.63	.88	1.28	.46	.61	1.13	.35	.52
Milk, butter, cheese, and eggs, ...	1.70	.82	1.29	1.51	.21	.70	.98	.14	.45
Total animal food, .	3.00	1.48	2.17	2.79	.67	1.51	1.68	.54	.97
Vegetable food, . .	4.17	2.38	3.02	5.65	2.35	3.44	3.65	1.65	2.49
Total food, .	7.17	4.12	5.19	7.26	3.02	4.95	4.89	2.20	3.46
Costs of Food-Materials.	cts.	cts.	cts.	cts.	cts.	cts.	cts.	cts.	cts.
Meats, fish, etc., . .	24	6	11	18	6	11	9	3	5
Milk, butter, cheese, and eggs, ...	12	4	6	11	3	5	7	1	3
Total animal food, .	36	10	17	29	10	16	13	5	8
Vegetable food, . .	11	6	8	13	6	8	8	5	6
Total food, .	47	16	25	39	17	24	19	11	14
Nutrients in Food-Materials.	lbs.	lbs.	lbs.	lbs.	lbs.	lbs.	lbs.	lbs.	lbs.
Protein, ...	.40	.21	.28	.44	.18	.26	.33	.16	.24
Fats, ...	.56	.29	.41	.67	.28	.45	.39	.16	.24
Carbohydrates, . .	1.36	1.05	1.17	1.75	.72	1.21	1.59	.85	1.16
Total nutrients, .	2.32	1.56	1.86	2.86	1.52	1.92	2.29	1.20	1.64
Percentages of animal protein in total protein of food, . .	per ct. 64	per ct. 47	per ct. 57	per ct. 62	per ct. 33	per ct. 46	per ct. 48	per ct 29	per ct. 37

DISCUSSION OF ANALYSES.

The figures contained in the tables, with the details upon which they are based, afford material for far more extended discussion than our limits warrant. Attention is called to a few points, however, which ought not to be overlooked.

In the following table the averages of the analyses of dietaries are succinctly set forth.

---

* The figures for "maximum" and "minimum" indicate the largest and smallest quantities, and those for "average," the averages, of all the dietaries of each series. Thus the largest quantity of meats, per man per day in any of the dietaries of Series A was 1.36 lbs., the smallest 0.63 lbs., and the average of the 7 dietaries of this series examined was 0.88 lbs. That the figures for "total" do not always equal the corresponding sum (for instance, the "Total animal food," maximum, series A, is less than the sum of the figures for meats, fish, etc., and for milk, butter, cheese, and eggs) is due to the fact that the factors which would make up the sum are from different dietaries, while the figures for "total" are the maximum, minimum, etc., for individual dietaries.

Averages of Analyses of Dietaries. Quantities and Costs of Foods and Quantities of Nutrients as estimated per Man per Day.

QUANTITIES, COSTS, AND NUTRIENTS OF FOOD-MATERIALS.	Miscellaneous, Massachusetts.	French Canadian.	
		Massachusetts.	Canada.
Quantities of Food-Materials.	lb.	lb.	lb.
Animal, ...	2.17	1.51	.97
Vegetable, ...	3.02	3.44	2.49
Total, ...	5.19	4.95	3.46
Costs of Food-Materials.	cts.	cts.	cts.
Animal, ...	17	16	8
Vegetable, ...	8	8	6
Total, ...	25	24	14
Nutrients in Food-Materials.	grams.	grams.	grams.
Protein, ...	127	118	109
Fats, ...	186	204	109
Carbohydrates, ...	531	549	527
Total, ...	844	871	745
Parts of animal protein in 100 of total protein, ...	per cent. 57	per cent. 46	per cent. 37

From this table it appears that the French Canadian laboring man whose food we have examined consumes at home three and one-half pounds of food (including milk) per day. But when he comes to Massachusetts and works in a factory or engages in other manual labor, he consumes five pounds, while other laborers, factory operatives, mechanics, etc., in Massachusetts, whose dietaries have been examined, consume five and one-fifth pounds of food per man per day. The food of the French Canadian at home costs fourteen cents but in Massachusetts he expends twenty-four cents, while the food of the other Massachusetts laborers costs twenty-five cents per day. The nutrients in the food-materials show corresponding gradations, the Canadian having one hundred and nine grams of protein per day at home and one hundred and eighteen in Massachusetts, while the other Massachusetts laborers have one hundred and twenty-seven grams. The gradations in the carbohydrates are similar, save that the differences are smaller. The amount of fats is smallest in the dietary of the Canadian in Canada, but nearly the same in those of the Canadian and other laborers in Massachusetts. That the Canadian in Massachusetts should have more fat than other laborers while he has so much less protein is apparently due to the larger proportion of salt pork in his meat.

Perhaps the most interesting fact set forth in this table is found in the proportions of animal and vegetable food. In Canada the French Canadian has one pound of animal food — meats, fish, milk, butter, cheese, eggs, etc. ; in Massachusetts he has a pound and a half, while his fellow-laborers of other nationalities have two and one-fifth pounds per man per day. There is a corresponding variation in the proportion of animal protein to the total protein of the food, the French Canadian at home having thirty-seven per cent, the same man in Massachusetts forty-six per cent, and other Massachusetts laborers fifty-seven per cent.

These figures are the expression of what we suppose to be a general law, namely, that where the conditions of life are otherwise approximately similar as in the different countries of Europe and America, not only the total amount of food, but, more especially, the amount of meat and other animal food consumed increases with the revenue of the consumer. We regret that corresponding statistics for laboring people in the different countries of Europe are not at hand, but feel confident that the outcome would sustain the proposition just made. It is a very familiar observation of those who have noted the habits of the ordinary people in European countries like Italy, Germany, and France, that the amounts of meat they consume are very small, and statistics show that their food is very apt to be deficient in protein.

In this connection it will be worth while to note briefly the results of some examinations of dietaries made in Middletown, Conn., a few months since. The figures are given as computed by Mr. I. S. Haynes, a member of the last graduating class of Wesleyan University, who, being interested in physiological chemistry, supplemented his regular work in the laboratory by some special studies which included, with the rest, examinations of dietaries of a students' club in the college and of the workmen employed in a brickyard not far from the city.

DIETARY OF STUDENTS IN MIDDLETOWN, CONN.

A large number of the students in Wesleyan University board in clubs. The club, which may have any number of members up to thirty, chooses one of its number as steward and arranges with a matron to cook and serve the food which he purchases. Many of the members having to pay their way through college, the majority are obliged and the rest are content to have the cost of their board made low even at the sacrifice of delicacies. While their diet is substantial and wholesome they regard it as plain and economical. They are mostly from the Eastern States and, coming from the class of families whose sons go to college, it seems fair to assume that their habits of eating formed at home would not differ materially from those of the more intelligent classes of people in that part of the country. While the habits of many are sedentary rather than active, they, nevertheless, take considerable muscular exercise. Out of two hundred sometimes seventy may be seen at once on the campus playing tennis and base ball. They are given to athletic sports in pleasant weather and many of them make use of the gymnasium in winter. They could hardly be credited with as much muscular exercise on the average as the laboring man doing moderate work, for whom standard rations are calculated, and they would, therefore, without doubt require somewhat less of protein as well as of the other nutrients in their food.

Mr. Haynes has taken the accounts of one of these clubs for a term of three months, and computed the amounts of the several kinds of food-materials purchased, and the quantities of nutrients in each and in the whole. He has then taken the number of days' board for which this food sufficed and thus calculated the average quantities of nutrients per day for each man to be:

Protein, 161 grams; Fats, 204 grams; Carbohydrates, 681 grams.

These figures are, perhaps, excessive, since they represent what the students paid for rather than the amounts actually consumed. The steward and some of the members of the club are of the opinion, however, that the amount of waste, that is to say, the material thrown away, was very small.

" All the meat and other available food that was not actually
served to the men at the table," said the steward, " was
carefully saved and made over into hash and croquettes."
Indeed, for that matter, " men who work their way through
college cannot afford to throw away their food. It costs too
much." But on investigating the matter more closely it ap-
peared that a portion of the material served was left upon the
plates and found its way into the garbage barrel or was given
to an indigent colored woman, who came for it regularly. At
Mr. Haynes' suggestion the steward had the amounts rejected
during one week weighed, and an estimate of its composition
was made by them. If we take this estimate of the waste
food of a week as a basis for the waste of the term, and assume
that the rest was actually eaten, the daily consumption will be
as follows :

CLASSIFICATION.	Protein.	Fats.	Carbohy-drates.
	Grams.	Grams.	Grams.
Purchased, ...	161	204	681
Thrown away, ...	13	19	-
Consumed, ...	148	185	681

DIETARY OF BRICKMAKERS IN MIDDLETOWN, CONN.

The proprietor of a brick yard in Middletown has furnished
an estimate of the total amount of food-materials furnished to
his men in a day. This Mr. Haynes computes to contain
nutrients per man per day as follows :

Protein, 222 grams ; Fats, 263 grams ; Carbohydrates, 758
grams.

The laborers to whom this extraordinary amount of food was
supplied were ordinary Canadians, Irishmen, and some native
Americans. Their work is rather trying, but the proprietor
makes it a point to secure good workmen, and finds one of the
best means of doing so is to " give them good board, which
they think more of than anything else." He assures us that
this is nearly all actually eaten, very little being thrown away.
He says that he sometimes gets freshly arrived immigrants at
Castle Garden, New York, and that he always finds they have
been accustomed to eat little or no meat, and adds : " They

come to me in very poor condition, but it is wonderful to see how they pick up, even with their hard work."

Comparison with European Dietaries.

That these dietaries give a complete representation of the quality or quantity of the food consumed by all classes of people is, of course, not claimed. The dietaries are those of persons, nearly all of whom work for wages and most for very little. While it is presumable that persons in more affluent circumstances pay for larger amounts of food and especially for larger proportions of meats and delicacies, whether they consume what they pay for or not, extended inquiries would be necessary to find out the actual facts. At the same time it is believed that these figures give a fair exhibit of the amounts and kinds of food ordinarily used by the laboring classes in the localities stated.

A proper estimate of the economy and fitness of these dietaries for their purpose will be facilitated by comparing them with dietaries of people in European countries whose conditions of life are such as to compel more rigid economy, and with standards based upon careful investigation as to the quantities of nutrients required for healthful nourishment. In the table which follows, such a comparison is made. The figures for European dietaries are collated by Playfair, Voit, and other well-known authorities. The standards are those mentioned in one of the preceding sections of this article.

Comparison of Dietaries Examined with European Dietaries and Standards.

DIETARIES.	NUTRIENTS PER DAY.		
	Protein.	Fats.	Carbo-hydrates.
American.	Grams.	Grams.	Grams.
French Canadians, working people, Canada (average),	109	109	527
French Canadians, factory operatives, mechanics, etc., Mass. (average),	118	204	549
Other factory operatives, mechanics, etc., Mass. (average),	127	186	531
Factory operatives, dressmakers, and clerks (boarding house), Lynn (A 7),	114	150	522
Glass blower, East Cambridge (A 11),	95	132	481
Machinist, Boston (A 9),	182	254	617
Students' club, Middletown, { Food purchased,	161	204	681
{ Food actually consumed,	148	185	681
Brickmakers, Middletown,	222	263	758

Comparison of Dietaries Examined — Concluded.

DIETARIES.	NUTRIENTS PER DAY.		
	Protein.	Fats.	Carbohy-drates.
European.	Grams.	Grams.	Grams.
Sewing girl, London, England, 1863 (wages, 93 cents per week),	53	33	315
Farm laborer, Ireland,	92	42	519
Poorly paid laborer, Hildesheim, Germany (diet mostly potatoes),	86	13	610
Ordinary mechanic, Munich, Germany,	131	68	494
"Well fed" tailor, England,	131	39	624
"Well paid" mechanic, Munich, Germany,	151	54	479
Average for adults with moderate exercise, England,	120	40	530
Brewery laborer, at severe labor, Munich, Germany,	190	73	600
Lumberman, Bavarian forest,	112	309	691
German soldier, peace footing,	117	26	547
German soldier, war footing,	151	46	522
German soldier, war footing, extraordinary dietary,	191	63	607
Voit's standard for laborer at moderate work,	118	56	500
Voit's standard for laborer at severe work,	145	100	450

The figures presented in this table are so clear as hardly to need explanation. In comparing the American with European dietaries, one cannot fail to be struck with the abundance of nutritive material in the former. The fat in the food of factory operatives in Massachusetts is larger in quantity than in that of any but the most bountiful of the European dietaries. While the quantities of the nutrients in the American dietaries are very large, those of fat as compared with the European figures are little less than enormous. It is probable, however, that the comparison is unfair in one respect. The figures represent in general the quantities of food supplied, not those actually eaten by the consumer. The difference between food purchased and that eaten, in the European dietaries, would be, it is believed, very small; while in many of the American ones it would probably be relatively larger. It would be an interesting study in social statistics for any one, willing to undertake it, to find out how much of the food, which the different classes of Americans pay for, is thus wasted. It is the general impression that the quantities of food which are thrown away or sold to the soapman are very large. It would on that account be natural to say that a very considerable proportion of fat in the American dietaries here examined should be deducted in order to get at the amounts actually eaten. But, as has already been explained, a little examination of the chemistry of the subject will indicate that in the meats, which

furnish the larger quantity of fat, so much of the fat occurs in
particles either invisible or too small to be conveniently re-
moved by the knife at the table, that the quantities of fat left
upon the plate and thus rejected make at most but a small
quantity of the fat in the meat, and, of course, a still smaller
proportion of the whole amount in the food.   And since allowance is made in the calculations for that which would be left
with the butcher, the composition of the meats as actually sold
being taken as the basis for the computation, any reasonable
allowance for rejection of fat in this way would be equivalent
to only a small quantity of the total amount in the dietary.
In other words, the conclusion is unavoidable that the actual
consumption of fat in our American dietaries is very large.

Even with the largest allowance that could reasonably be
made for waste of nutrients, the amounts which must be consumed of the dietaries here studied are in many cases very
large indeed as compared with the European dietaries and
standards.   As was stated in one of the preceding sections,
the best results of research in the science of nutrition imply
that a certain minimum quantity of protein is requisite for
healthful nourishment and that all the protein above this shares
with the carbohydrates and fats the function which may be
roughly designated as serving for fuel, and that in this respect
one pound by weight of fat is equivalent to two pounds or
more either of protein or carbohydrates.   The excessive quantities of fats in the American dietaries, therefore, made their
nutritive power much larger as compared with the European
dietaries than the figures taken by themselves would imply.
In other words, the American dietaries contain, in general, not
only excessively large quantities of food, but the particular
kinds of nutrients, namely, fats, which weight for weight do
the most work in the body, are the ones which are the most
largely in excess.

IMPROVEMENTS IN DIETARIES.

As has been urged, the American dietaries here examined
contain much larger amounts of food than are judged appropriate by those who have paid most attention to the study of
the subject, a fact which is brought very clearly into view by
comparing the American dietaries with the European standards
in the preceding table.   In general the excess seems to be due

to the meats and sweetmeats. In his examination of the
students' dietaries above cited, Mr. Haynes has calculated that
if one-half of the meats, dairy products, sugar, and apples and
all the honey and tapioca had been left out and the rest
properly utilized, the food would have still exceeded Voit's
standard. His figures, condensed, are as below:

CLASSIFICATION.	Protein.	Fats.	Carbohydrates.
Total purchased, ...	Grams. 161	Grams. 204	Grams. 681
One-half of all the meats, milk, cheese, and eggs; one-half of all the sugar, molasses, and apples, and all the honey and tapioca together contained, ...	43	97	127
The remaining food-materials supplied, ...	118	107	554
Voit's standard for a laboring man, ...	118	56	500

That is to say, according to these figures, the young men of
this club might have dispensed with one-half their meat and
one-half their dessert and still have had more nutritive material
in their food than the German standard requires for a laboring
man at moderate work. Somewhat similar calculations have
been made for two of the Massachusetts dietaries.

One of these, No. A 9, was that of a family in Boston, consisting of husband and wife. The husband is a machinist and
earns nineteen and one-half dollars a week. The dietary furnishes seven and one-half pounds of food (including milk)
and costs forty-seven cents per man per day. The following
computation shows how the dietary might have been altered:

Suggestions for the Alteration of Dietary A 9.

DESCRIPTION.	FOOD-MATERIALS.			NUTRIENTS.		
	Prices per lb.	Quantities.	Costs.	Protein.	Fats.	Carbohydrates.
If from the dietary, which furnishes per man per day, .	cents. –	lbs. 7.17	$0 47	lbs. .40	lbs. .56	lbs. 1.36
Or, for 1.8 men in 30 days, .	–	387.6	25 38	21.5	29.8	73.5
We take out— Two-thirds of the meats, fish, etc.,	–	49	$8 46	6.0	11.0	–
One-half of the dairy products and eggs, ...	–	44.4	3 25	2.1	5.6	1.8
One-half of the sugar and molasses, . . .	–	9.8	74	–	–	9.3
Total deducted, ...	. .	103.2	$12 45	8.1	16.6	11.1
There will remain, . . .	. .	284.4	$12 93	13.4	13.2	62.4
Or, per man per day, . . .	. .	5.27	24	.25	.24	1.15
Voit's standard, ...	. .	–	–	.26	.12	1.10

In other words, if two-thirds of the meats and fish, one-half the dairy products and eggs, and one-half of the sugar and molasses had been omitted and the rest carefully utilized, the dietary would still have exceeded our standard in its amounts of nutrients, and the cost of the food would have been reduced one-half.

In the other, No. A 11, that of the family of a glass-blower in Cambridge, earning three and one-half dollars per day, the estimated quantity of food (including milk) was four and one-half pounds, costing twenty-five cents per man per day. The quantity of protein was rather smaller than our standard calls for, but the amount of fats was more than double that of the same standard. By taking in the place of the most expensive kinds of beefsteak the cheaper but no less wholesome round steak and shin, and in the place of one-half the lamb and three-fourths the salt pork and lard, substituting codfish and haddock, the amount of protein would be increased and that of the fats reduced to the standard, and about one-sixth of the cost would be saved.

Suggestions for the Alteration of Dietary A 11.

DESCRIPTION.	FOOD-MATERIALS.			NUTRIENTS.		
	Prices per lb.	Quantities.	Costs.	Protein.	Fats.	Carbohydrates.
If from the dietary which furnishes per man per day, .	cents.	lbs. 4.45	$0 25	lbs. .21	lbs. 29	lbs. 1.06
Or, for 12.6 men in 30 days, .	–	142.30	7 99	6.80	9.40	34.10
We take out—						
The whole of the beef steak, .	28	6.0	$1 68	0.8	1.0	–
One-half of the lamb, .	15	2 5	38	0.4	0.6	–
Three-fourths of the salt pork,	10	0.8	08	–	0.6	–
Three-fourths of the lard, .	10	0.7	07	–	0.7	–
One-half the dairy products and eggs, .	–	13.1	1 11	0.6	2.3	0.6
Total deducted, . .	. .	23.1	$3 32	1.8	5.2	0.6
There will remain, . . .	–	119.2	$4 67	5.0	4.2	33.5
To which may be added—						
Beef shin, ...	5	6.0	$0 25	0.7	0.1	–
Beef steak, round, . .	18	4.0	72	0.7	0.4	–
Fresh codfish, . . .	10	5.0	50	0.6	–	–
Fresh haddock, . . .	7	5.0	35	0.4	–	–
Salt codfish, . . .	5	5 0	25	0.8	–	–
Total added, . .	. .	24 0	$2 07	3.2	0.5	–
There will then be, .	. .	143.2	$6 74	8.2	4.7	33.5
Or, per man per day, .	. .	4.48	21	.26	.15	1.05
Voit's standard, . .	. .	. .	. .	.26	.12	1.10

It is by no means claimed that the changes indicated in these calculations are exactly the ones which should be made. The proper adjustment of the dietary is a matter of convenience and palatability as well as chemical composition, but the figures cited will suffice to show that there is great room for improvement.

FOOD OF THE POOR IN BOSTON.

That the rich man becomes richer by saving and the poor man poorer by wasting his money is one of the commonest facts of daily experience. It is a fact too, with a pathetic side, for very often those who suffer most from want and are at the same time most anxious to economize are least able to do so. One great difficulty is that they do not understand how to save.

The agents of the Bureau in collecting the statistics of dietaries of series " A " have made inquiries of tradesmen as to the kinds of food the poor of Boston purchase and the prices they pay. Some of the results of these inquiries are as follows :

By poor people is meant those who earn just enough to keep themselves and families from want. When a groceryman or marketman is asked, " What is your experience in dealing with your poor customers in regard to the quality of food used by them ? " the answer is, in almost every case, " Oh, they usually want the best and pay for it and the most fastidious are those who can least afford it."

In the matter of beef, for instance, the cuts most used for steak are the face of the round, costing from 18 to 20 cents per pound; the tip of the sirloin at from 20 to 25 cents, and rib roast at from 18 to 20 cents. They do not use the flank piece for steak, and would feel insulted if it were offered to them. The flour they use is the best. For butter they pay from 28 to 30 cents per pound at present prices. All their other groceries are such as are sold to first-class customers.

One man told his butcher that hard times were owing to the meanness of the rich and the extravagance of the poor, and that the poor helped make themselves so in the way they did their buying. They send their children after a pound of lard and take it home in a paper. The loss, even in this, is of some consequence to them in a year. A marketman who was much interested in this investigation referred to the following newspaper extract as coinciding with his experience:

" A woman stepped into one of the best class provision stores of Boston a few days since and called for a cut of ' tenderloin steak.' Now a tenderloin of beef is a very toothsome article of food, and no person need be blamed for valuing the enjoyment arising from its qualities of flavor and tenderness. But, as the price of this commodity ranges all the way from 40 to 75 cents per pound in these markets, it must be classed among luxuries by the average purchaser, and the customer above alluded to was well known to be a hard-working person, earning her living by a good deal of sweating of the brow, and constantly finding necessities hard enough to procure, let alone luxuries — in short, she was a washerwoman. In this instance the disproportion between ability and desire was so great and so evident that the marketman could not help suggesting that he had other ' cuts ' of beef equally nutritious and tasteful, and which could be afforded at a moiety of the price charged for tenderloin. The advice was rejected, with strong signs of resentment, and the tenderloin was bought and paid for.

" This transaction illustrates completely what is going on all the time in our communities, the woeful lack of consistency and appreciation in economical relations, and to how great extent folly and pride constitute elements in daily life and living. In the experiences of tradesmen who furnish the wherewithal to sustain human existence it is being repeated over and over again every day ; and the class represented by this poor woman is by no means the only one affected. As to the underlying causes upon which such transactions are based, investigation reveals a curious foundation made up of pride, ignorance and indifference."

That the above statements mean more than appears at first glance will be seen from a few moments' consideration.

This washerwoman had her choice between, let us suppose, tenderloin at 40 cents, sirloin at 25 cents, round at 15 cents, and neck or shoulder at 8 cents per pound. Aside from gratification of pride or palate there is no advantage in purchasing tenderloin ; the other pieces are just as nutritious and wholesome. The proper use of meat in nutrition is to furnish fat and especially protein. So far as the protein is concerned one part of the beef is as valuable for nourishment as another. Supposing these different pieces to have been of the usual composition, the costs of protein would have been somewhat as follows :

Costs of Protein per Pound.

In neck	at 8 cents per pound,	.	.	.	$0 33
In round	" 15 " " "	.	.	.	59
In sirloin	" 25 " " "	.	.	.	1 06
In tenderloin	" 40 " " "	.	.	.	2 40

That is to say, this good washerwoman paid four times as much for the protein in tenderloin as she need have paid if she had taken round steak and more than seven times as much as if she had been content with neck or shoulder.

Or, to put it in another way, if instead of taking the pound of tenderloin she had been content with a pound of round steak she would have got just about the same quantity of nutritive material. It would have been somewhat less tender and tooth-some but just as nutritious and she would have saved 25 cents of her hard earned money ; and if she had taken the neck or shoulder which suffice for many a rich man's table the saving would have been still greater.

Another Boston butcher gives an account of his experience which accords exactly with the statements above quoted. He had often talked with poor people about this matter and found them generally very firm in their conviction that the dearest meats are the most nutritious and hence the most economical. He insisted particularly on the fact that while the ignorant poor invest their money so unwisely, many of his wealthy customers were in the habit of taking the coarser pieces which the poor refused. It is the old story of the economy of the rich and the wastefulness of the poor.

Part of the evil at least is due to ignorance. There can be no more truly Christian form of charity than the helping of worthy but uninformed people of limited incomes by instructing them how to economize in the purchase as well as in the use of their food. The most effective charity is that which helps the recipients to help themselves.

Some of the most interesting figures regarding the costs and quantities of food-materials in the Massachusetts and Canadian dietaries may be concisely summarized. It will be remembered that Series A, Miscellaneous, Massachusetts, includes dietaries of factory and mill operatives, mechanics, and a few clerks, dressmakers, etc., of various nationalities, in Lowell, Lawrence, Lynn, East Cambridge, and Boston. Series B, French Canadians, Massachusetts, includes factory operatives and a few mechanics of Canadian origin, working in Massachusetts. Series C, French Canadians, Canada, includes similar people, mainly or entirely laboring classes in Canada.

The costs of the total food, per man per day, in the different dietaries as set forth in the tables, were:

SERIES.	Maximum.	Minimum.	Average.
	cents.	cents.	cents.
Miscellaneous, Massachusetts, ...	47	16	25
French Canadians, Massachusetts, . . .	30	17	24
French Canadians, Canada, ...	19	11	14

The costs of the animal food, the meats, fish, dairy products and eggs, were:

SERIES.	Maximum.	Minimum.	Average.
	cents.	cents.	cents.
Miscellaneous, Massachusetts, . . .	36	10	17
French Canadians, Massachusetts, . . .	29	10	16
French Canadians, Canada, . . .	13	5	8

The total quantities of food, including milk, per man per day, were:

SERIES.	Maximum.	Minimum.	Average.
	lbs.	lbs.	lbs.
Miscellaneous, Massachusetts, . . .	7.17	4.12	5.19
French Canadians, Massachusetts, . .	7.26	3.02	4.95
French Canadians, Canada, . . .	4.89	2.20	3.46

The total quantities of animal food were:

SERIES.	Maximum.	Minimum.	Average.
	lbs.	lbs.	lbs.
Miscellaneous, Massachusetts, ...	3.00	1.43	2.17
French Canadians, Massachusetts, . .	2.79	0.67	1.51
French Canadians, Canada, . . .	1.68	0.54	0.97

The proportions of animal protein in total protein were :

SERIES.	Maximum.	Minimum.	Average.
	Per cent.	Per cent.	Per cent.
Miscellaneous, Massachusetts, . . .	64	47	57
French Canadians, Massachusetts, . . .	62	33	46
French Canadians, Canada, . . .	48	29	37

The total quantities of nutrients (protein, fats, and carbo-hydrates), expressed in hundredths of a pound, were :

SERIES.	Maximum.	Minimum.	Average.
	lbs.	lbs.	lbs.
Miscellaneous, Massachusetts, . . .	2.32	1.56	1.86
French Canadians, Massachusetts, . . .	2.86	1.52	1.92
French Canadians, Canada, . . .	2.29	1.20	1.64

Among the most noticeable features of the dietaries exam-ined are :

1. The very large quantities of food, especially in the dietaries of factory and mill operatives, mechanics, and other people engaged in manual labor in Massachusetts and Con-necticut.

2. The very large amounts of animal food, especially in the dietaries just mentioned.

3. The quantities of fat, which are large in nearly all and extremely large in many of the dietaries. The fat comes mostly from the meats, especially pork, and from butter and lard.

The quantities of total nutrients and of fats are the more striking when compared with those of the European dietaries, as is done in the table on pages 315 and 316, *ante*. Thus the total weight of nutrients per man per day varies in the Massachu-setts dietaries from 690 grams (1.52 pounds) to 1,053 grams (2.32 pounds), while in the European dietaries the range is from 401 to 1,112 grams, or, omitting the dietaries of the London sewing girl and the Bavarian lumberman as very exceptional and abnormal, from 653 to 863 grams. The fats in the European dietaries, omitting the case of the Bavarian lumberman, range from 13 to 100 grams, though in some instances not here quoted they somewhat exceed 100. In the Massachusetts dietaries the amount of fat is in no case less than 127 and reaches, in one instance, 304 grams. If common usage in Europe and the standards which are currently accepted there are correct expressions of the proper quantities of food and of fat for healthful nutrition, the quantities of total food, of meats, and especially of fats in the dietaries here reported are in general needlessly large, and in some instances excessively so.

These data suggest numerous questions such as:

1. How much more food of the American than of the European dietaries is wasted, that is, not eaten?

2. How much superiority of the American workingman is due to his more liberal diet?

3. How much injury is done to health by over-eating in this country?

In brief, the dietaries thus studied all point in one direction and indicate that in this country a large excess of food is consumed not only by well-to-do people, but also by those in moderate circumstances, mechanics, operatives in mills and factories, etc.

The excess of food consists mainly of meats and sweetmeats. Common observation would imply that of this excess a considerable part is simply thrown away. But it can hardly be doubted that in many cases much more food than is needed is actually taken into the system. If the opinions of our best physiologists and physicians are to be accepted, this overloading of the alimentary organs is seriously injurious to health.

The animal foods are pecuniarily the most costly, as estimated by the amount of nutritive material which they furnish for a given sum of money. The expensiveness of the nutrients in the animal foods, together with the large excess, makes the use of meats and dairy products in such large quantities doubly uneconomical.

In numerous cases the dietaries could be so altered as to make them at once less expensive, equally wholesome and palatable, and much more healthful.

One of the most interesting and important facts of all is the very common practice of the poor to purchase the more expensive food-materials, especially meats, when food obtainable at only a fraction of the cost would be equally wholesome and nutritious.

If the further study of this matter should confirm these results, as there seems to be good ground to expect would be the case, it would become a serious question whether a reform in the dietary habits of a large portion of our people, including the classes who work for small wages, is not greatly needed, and whether this reform would not consist in many instances in the use of less food as a whole, and in many more cases in the use of relatively less meat and larger proportions of vegetable foods.

www.ingramcontent.com/pod-product-compliance
Lightning Source LLC
Chambersburg PA
CBHW020037030726
47499CB00007B/2477